MW00559123

Confusing
Science Terms

BY
SCHYRLET CAMERON AND CAROLYN CRAIG

COPYRIGHT © 2009 Mark Twain Media, Inc.

ISBN 978-1-58037-511-5

Printing No. CD-404114

Mark Twain Media, Inc., Publishers
Distributed by Carson-Dellosa Publishing LLC

Visit us at www.carsondellosa.com

Table of Contents

Introduction to the Teacher

Confusing Science Terms promotes student knowledge and understanding of science concepts through vocabulary building. As science education reform continues to be a priority for our nation, teachers are striving to create learning environments that encourage scientific literacy. Students must understand the written text in order to learn new science concepts. Providing vocabulary instruction is one of the most significant ways a teacher can advance student understanding and academic achievement in science.

Confusing Science Terms concentrates on commonly confused word pairs, word triplets, and perplexing science terminology. Chapters are organized to allow students to learn those confusing words associated with physical, life, and earth and space science. Each section provides students with correct word pronunciation and syllabication, reader-friendly text, and clear and explicit graphics.

The teaching strategy described in this book promotes differentiated instruction. Vocabulary-building activities provide multiple opportunities for students to learn the language of science. Teachers may choose to focus on decoding and word meaning for English-language learners and reluctant readers. Alternative methods of instruction such as hands-on activities, small group work, games, and journaling target multiple learning styles and help learners at all levels.

Confusing Science Terms supports the No Child Left Behind (NCLB) Act. The activities found in this book were designed to strengthen scientific literacy skills and were correlated to the National Science Education Standards (NSES). National and state science standards, science textbooks, and Mark Twain Media science publications were reviewed in an effort to identify those words that are confusing because they look alike, sound alike, or seem alike. Language building strategies recommended by researchers (Curtis and Long: 2001, Marzano and Pickering: 2005) were evaluated to determine the most effective approach for teaching and learning vocabulary.

National Standards

National Science Education Standards (NSES)
National Research Council (1996). *National Science Education Standards.* Washington, D.C.: National Academy Press.

Science as Inquiry
Content Standard A: As a result of activities in grades 5–8, all students should develop:
- abilities necessary to do scientific inquiry.
- understanding about scientific inquiry.

Physical Science
Content Standard B: As a result of activities in grades 5–8, all students should develop an understanding of:
- properties of objects and materials.
- motions and of forces.
- transfer of energy.

Life Science
Content Standard C: As a result of activities in grades 5–8, all students should develop an understanding of:
- structure and function in living systems.
- reproduction and heredity.
- populations and ecosystems.
- diversity and adaptations of organisms.

Earth and Space Science
Content Standard D: As a result of activities in grades 5–8, all students should develop an understanding of:
- structure of the earth system.
- Earth's history.
- Earth in the solar system.

How to Use This Book

Teaching science vocabulary before content will help students build an understanding of the concepts to be taught. The Association for Supervision and Curriculum Development and the International Reading Association both support using a systematic approach to teaching vocabulary.

Vocabulary Strategies
- Focus on science words with similar pronunciations, spellings, and meanings that seem confusing to students.
- Use a science vocabulary journal or notebook. Students construct their own meaning, write a sentence, and create a visual representation of the word in their journal.

Word	Definition	Picture
	Sentence	

Steps for Presenting a Lesson From the Book

Step #1 – Confused Thinking Introduce Words
- A one-sentence explanation of why the terms are often confused.

Step #2 – Straight Talk Construct Meaning
- The word definitions and explanations are presented in an easy-to-read format. **Bolded words** correspond with **key words** to shorten lengthy definitions.

Step #3 – Example A Closer Look at the Words
- The terms are used in an easy-to-understand context that students can relate to.

Step #4 – Apply Reinforcement
- A word-related science activity allows students to apply what they have learned.

Step #5 – Check Yourself Assessment
- A quick 10-question quiz at the end of each section checks for mastery.

Other Lesson Features: Information boxes appear randomly throughout the book.

Word Clue	Amazing Fact	Memory Trick
Prefix/suffix, root words, or parts of speech bolded with shortened meaning.	*Bolded key term* used in a fact of interest.	A *simple way* to remember science terms.

Science Journal

Directions: Copy the word, write the definition in your own words, use the word in a sentence, and draw a picture illustrating the word. Collect all your science journal pages in a binder or folder to use as a reference.

Word	Definition	Picture
	Sentence	
Word	Definition	Picture
	Sentence	
Word	Definition	Picture
	Sentence	
Word	Definition	Picture
	Sentence	
Word	Definition	Picture
	Sentence	

a lap   ā lane   e bet   ē be   i kit   ī ice   o hot   ō old   u cut   o͞o fruit

Pronunciation Key

a	lap, pat, mad		o	hot, top, odd
ā	lane, age, hay		ō	old, toad, know, toe
ä	father, yarn, ah		oi	oil, toy
âr	care, hair		ô	law, caught, for, horse, off, order
e	bet, end, hen, said		o͞o	book, pull, should
ē	bee, equal, piece, real		o͞o	fruit, glue, food, few
ər	better, perfect, baker		ou	out, cow, house
ə	about, taken, pencil, come, circus		sh	she, dish, machine
hw	when, whether, nowhere		th	thin, both
i	kit, in		*th*	this, mother, smooth
ī	ice, my, line, cried		u	cut, up
îr	ear, deer, here, pierce		ûr	fur, term, bird, word, learn

What Is a Pronunciation Key?

A pronunciation key is a list of symbols and familiar key words that contain the sound represented by the symbols. The system used in this book was especially designed to make it easier for you to read and understand the written pronunciations for words. Place a copy of the key above in your science journal or notebook as a quick reference for the pronunciation symbols used in this book.

Using a Pronunciation Key

- Symbols are used to represent the sounds used in the pronunciation of a word.
- Hyphens (-) are used to separate the pronunciations into syllables.
- **Boldface** letters are used to indicate the part of the word to be stressed or spoken with the greatest force.

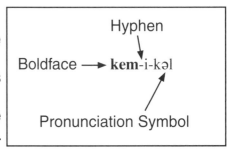

Check Yourself

Use the pronunciation key above to answer the questions.

1. How many syllables does the word *photosynthesis* (fō-tō-**sin**-thi-sis) have? _____

2. Which syllable is stressed in the word *diffusion* (dif-**yo͞o**-zhən)? _____

3. Which word in the pronunciation key helps you pronounce the /oi/ sound heard in the word *buoyancy* (**boi**-ən-sē)? _____

4. Which word in the pronunciation key helps you pronounce the second syllable in the word *monocot* (**mon**-ə-kot)? _____

5. Which word in the pronunciation key helps you pronounce the /ûr/ sound in the word *current* (**kûr**-ənt)? _____

Matter

atomic mass / atomic number

Confused Thinking The words atomic mass (ə-**tom**-ik **mas**) and atomic number (ə-**tom**-ik **num**-bər) are often confused because both terms are numbers in the Periodic Table of Elements that give specific information about the structure of an atom.

atomic number

name of element

11
Na
Sodium
22.990

symbol

atomic mass

Straight Talk The Periodic Table of Elements is a chart listing all the known elements. Each box in the table displays information about an atom of one of the 112 elements. The **atomic number** represents the **number of protons** in the nucleus of the atom. The **atomic mass** (sometimes called atomic weight) represents the **average mass of one atom of the element,** which includes the **protons, neutrons, and electrons**.

Example In the Periodic Table of the Elements, the atomic number for sodium is 11. The atomic mass of sodium is 22.990.

Apply Record the atomic number and atomic mass of each element.

13	8	2
Al	**O**	**He**
Aluminum	Oxygen	Helium
26.982	**15.999**	**4.003**

atomic number 1. _____ 2. _____ 3. _____

atomic mass   _____   _____   _____

chemical bond / covalent bond / ionic bond

Confused Thinking The words chemical bond (**kem**-i-kəl **bond**), covalent bond (kō-**vā**-lənt **bond**), and ionic bond (ī-**on**-ik **bond**) are confusing because the way these bonds are formed is not understood.

Straight Talk The elements in a compound are held together by chemical bonds, so **chemical bond** is the overall term for the attraction holding together the atoms of compounds. There are two main types of chemical bonds. An **ionic bond** is formed when **atoms transfer electrons**. A **covalent bond** is formed when **atoms share electrons**.

Example Salt is an example of an ionic bond. A sodium atom transfers an electron to a chlorine atom.

Apply Below is a water molecule. What type of bond is formed between the hydrogen and oxygen atoms? Explain.

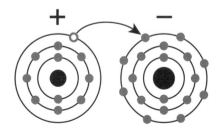

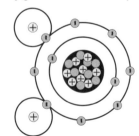

_____

_____

_____

_____

_____

Matter

---

element / molecule / compound

Confused Thinking The words element (el-ə-mənt), molecule (mol-i-kyōōl), and compound (kom-pound) are confusing because the relationships among the three are not understood.

Straight Talk An **element** is a substance **made of the same type of atoms**. A **compound** is formed when **two or more different elements join** together chemically. A **molecule** is the **smallest unit** of a compound.

Example Table salt is a compound formed by the elements sodium (Na) and chlorine (Cl). The elements form molecules which can be written as chemical formulas using the symbols for the two elements: NaCl. The molecule NaCl is the smallest unit of the compound known as table salt.

Apply Complete the data table below. Classify each example as an element, compound, or molecule. In your own words, write a definition for each term.

Example	Type of Matter	Definition
1. H_2O		
2. Ne		
3. water		

---

mass / weight

Confused Thinking The words mass (mas) and weight (wāt) are often confused because the terms are used interchangeably in everyday language, but there is a distinct difference between the two terms in science.

Straight Talk **Mass** is a measurement of the **amount of matter** (stuff) in an object. **Weight** is the measurement of the **pull of gravity** on an object. Every time you weigh yourself on a scale, you are measuring the pull of the Earth's gravity on you. The mass of an object doesn't change when an object moves from place to place, but weight does.

Example The balance scale is used to measure the mass of an object in grams.

A spring scale is used to measure the weight of an object in newtons.

Apply What would happen to the weight and mass of a person if he or she went from Earth to the moon? Explain your answer. _____

_____

Matter

neutron / proton / electron

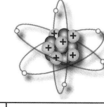

Confused Thinking The words neutron (**nōō**-tron), proton (**prō**-ton), and electron (i-**lek**-tron) are confusing terms because the structure of an atom is complicated and difficult to picture.

Straight Talk Matter is made of atoms. An atom is made up of electrons, protons, and neutrons. The **nucleus of an atom** is made of two kinds of particles: **protons** and **neutrons**. Protons have a positive charge, and neutrons are neutral, having no charge. **Electrons** have a negative charge, and they **circle the nucleus** of the atom.

Example

Particle	Charge	Location
proton	positive (+)	nucleus
neutron	neutral (no charge)	nucleus
electron	negative (-)	electron cloud

Apply Create a 3-dimensional model of an atom that can be hung from a string. Select an element from the list below. Research the element. Use the information to make a detailed sketch of the atom. Make sure to display the correct number of neutrons, electrons, and protons; these should be in their correct locations. Next, decide what to use to represent the neutrons, electrons, and protons. Anything small and round that can be glued to each other will work, such as ping-pong or styrofoam balls. Color code the balls so that it is easier to identify the protons, neutrons, and electrons. The electrons should be smaller than the protons and neutrons.

Elements: hydrogen   sodium   copper   carbon   calcium   gold

 Check Yourself

Matching

1. _____ atomic number
2. _____ covalent bond
3. _____ element
4. _____ mass
5. _____ electron

a. a chemical bond formed when atoms share electrons
b. the number of protons in the nucleus of the atom
c. circles the nucleus of the atom
d. a measurement of the amount of matter in an object
e. a pure substance made of atoms of the same type

Fill in the Blanks

newtons   element   chemical   compound   nucleus

6. Hydrogen (H) is an example of a(n) _____ found on the Periodic Table.

7. Carbon dioxide (CO_2) is an example of a(n) _____.

8. A spring scale is used to measure the weight of an object in _____.

9. Protons and neutrons are both located in the _____ of an atom.

10. There are two main types of _____ bonds.

Chemistry

acid / base / neutral

Confused Thinking The words acid (**as**-id), base (**bās**), and neutral (**nōō**-trəl) are often confusing terms because the relationships among the three terms are not understood.

Straight Talk A pH scale is a tool for measuring acids and bases. The scale ranges from 0-14: Litmus paper is an indicator used to tell if a substance is an acid or a base. The color of the paper matches up with the numbers on the pH scale to indicate what kind of substance is being tested. A substance with **a pH of 7** is classified as a **neutral (neither acid nor base)**. A substance with **a pH below 7** is classified as an **acid**. A substance with **a pH above 7** is classified as a **base** (alkaline).

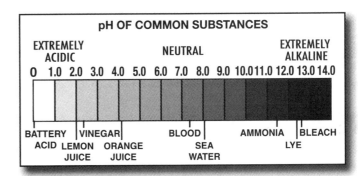

Example Vinegar is an acid and measures 2.4 on the pH scale. Bleach is a base and measures 12.6 on the pH scale. Water is a neutral substance and measures 7 on the pH scale.

Apply Test each substance with litmus paper. Complete the table by classifying each substance as acid, base, or neutral.

Substance	Acid	Base (alkaline)	Neutral
1. lemon juice			
2. milk			
3. ammonia			

carbon dioxide / carbon monoxide

Confused Thinking The words carbon dioxide (**kär**-bən dī-**ok**-sīd) and carbon monoxide (**kär**-bən mon-**ok**-sīd) are often confused because they have similar pronunciations and spellings, and they are both gases.

Straight Talk **Carbon dioxide** (CO_2) is a colorless, odorless, **non-poisonous gas**. **Carbon monoxide** (CO) is a colorless, odorless, **toxic gas**.

> **Word Clue**
>
> **di-** a prefix meaning **two.** Dioxide means two atoms of oxygen.
>
> **mon-** a prefix meaning **one.** Monoxide stands for one atom of oxygen.

Example Carbon dioxide is a natural part of the air. It is released by yeast during fermentation, during respiration in animals, and in the burning of fossil fuels. Carbon monoxide is a toxic gas that is released when any fuel such as gas, oil, kerosene, wood, or charcoal is burned. That's why you should always open a window or vent when lighting a fire in a fireplace in your home

Apply Place a package of dry yeast and two tablespoons of sugar in a beaker. Pour warm water into the beaker. Let the mixture sit for 10 minutes. Record your observations.

Chemistry

chemical change / physical change

Confused Thinking The words chemical change (**kem**-i-kəl **chānj**) and physical change (**fĭz**-i-kəl **chānj**) are often confused because they both describe a type of change in matter.

Straight Talk A **chemical change** occurs when one or more substances are **changed into a new substance** with different properties. A **physical change** occurs when a substance changes in size, shape, or form (solid, liquid, or gas) but **does not change its identity**.

Example A chemical change occurs when a candle is burned. New substances such as ash and smoke are formed, and energy in the form of heat is released. A physical change occurs when an apple is cut in half. Its size and shape changes, but not its identity. It is still an apple.

Apply Complete the data table below. Classify the type of change as chemical or physical.

Example	Type of Change
1. a lawn being mowed	
2. a bicycle rusting	
3. water freezing	
4. toast burning	

chemical equation / chemical formula

Confused Thinking The words chemical equation (**kem**-i-kəl i-kwā-zhən) and chemical formula (**kem**-i-kəl fôr-myə-lə) are often confused because they both use letters, numbers, and symbols instead of words.

Memory Trick
Math equation: $2 + 2 = 4$
Chemical equation: $2H_2 + O_2 \rightarrow 2H_2O$
Both use the "+" sign, meaning add.

Straight Talk A **chemical equation** is a shorthand way to **describe a chemical reaction** between two or more substances. A **chemical formula** is a shorthand way to **name the elements in a compound** and their proportions.

Example $2H_2 + O_2 \rightarrow 2H_2O$ is the chemical equation for water. The "+" sign means combine, and an arrow means "yield." $2H_2 + O_2 \rightarrow 2H_2O$ means four hydrogen atoms combine with two oxygen atoms to yield two molecules of water. H_2O is the chemical formula scientists use to represent the compound we call water.

Apply Complete the data table by classifying each example as a chemical equation or chemical formula.

Example	Chemical Equation / Chemical Formula
1. CO_2	
2. $H_2CO_3 \rightarrow H_2O + CO_2$	
3. $Fe + S \rightarrow FeS$	

Confusing Science Terms   Chapter 1—Physical Science

Chemistry

endothermic reaction / exothermic reaction

Confused Thinking The words endothermic (en-dō-**thûr**-mik) reaction and exothermic (ek-sō-**thûr**-mik) reaction are often confused because they have similar pronunciations and spellings, and they are both chemical reactions involving heat energy.

> **Word Clue**
> **endo-** a prefix meaning **within**
> **exo-** a prefix meaning **out of**

Straight Talk During an **endothermic reaction**, heat energy is **absorbed**, cooling the immediate surroundings. During an **exothermic reaction**, heat energy is **released,** causing the temperature of the immediate surroundings to rise.

Example Bread baking is an example of an endothermic reaction. A firecracker exploding is an example of an exothermic reaction.

Apply

1. What kind of reaction occurs when an egg is cooking?

_____

2. What kind of reaction occurs when a candle is burning?

_____

heterogeneous mixture / homogeneous mixture

Confused Thinking The words heterogeneous (het-ər-ə-**jē**-nē-əs) mixture and homogeneous (hō-mə-**jē**-nē-əs) mixture are often confused because they have similar pronunciations and spellings, and they are both mixtures.

> **Word Clue**
> **hetero-** a prefix meaning **different**
> **homo-** a prefix meaning **same**

Straight Talk A **heterogeneous mixture** is a substance in which you **can see** the different parts. A **homogeneous mixture** is a substance in which you **cannot see** the different parts.

Example Orange juice with pulp is a heterogeneous mixture. Air is a homogeneous mixture of many gases.

Apply Complete the data table below. Classify the mixture as homogeneous or heterogeneous.

Substance	Type of Mixture
1. salad	
2. salt water	
3. milk	
4. supreme pizza	

CD-404114 © Mark Twain Media, Inc., Publishers   11

Chemistry

soluble / dissolved

Confused Thinking The words soluble (säl-yə-bəl) and dissolved (di-**zälv**-əd) are confusing because the relationship between the two terms is not understood.

Straight Talk When a substance can totally mix with a liquid, it is **soluble**. A soluble substance is always soluble, even if it is not mixed with any liquid. When a soluble substance is totally mixed with the liquid, it has **dissolved**. Dissolved describes the state of a soluble substance totally mixing with a liquid.

Word Clue
soluble is an **adjective**
dissolved is a **verb**

Example Sugar is soluble in water, even when it is not mixed with water. When sugar is added to water, it completely mixes with the water. It has dissolved.

Apply Fill a clear glass beaker with tap water. Gently shake a packet of red or blue powdered fruit drink into the beaker. Observe the reaction of the powder as it enters the water. Continue adding powder to the beaker until the water is completely colored. Why did streams of red color streak through the water? _____

_____

_____

solute / solvent

Confused Thinking The words solute (sə-**lo͞ot**) and solvent (**sol**-vənt) are often confused because they have similar spellings and they are both parts of the same solution.

Straight Talk Solutions can be made up of different combinations of solids, liquids, and gases. A solution has two parts: a solute and a solvent. The **solute** is the substance that **dissolves**. The **solvent** is the **substance in which the solute dissolves.**

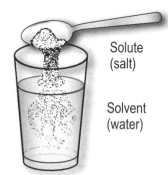

Solute (salt)

Solvent (water)

Example Salt water is a solution. Salt (the substance that dissolves) is the solute. Water (the substance in which the salt dissolves) is the solvent.

Apply Research the solutions below. Using that information, identify the solvent and the solute for each. Record the answers in the data table.

Solution	Solvent	Solute
1. carbonated beverage		
2. ocean water		
3. air		
4. brass		

Chemistry

solution / suspension

Confused Thinking The words solution (sə-**loo**-shən) and suspension (sə-**spen**-shən) are often confused because they are both mixtures.

Straight Talk A **solution** is a mixture in which the particles are **too small to see**. A **suspension** is a mixture in which the particles are **large enough to see**. Remember, suspensions are always temporary. The substances in a suspension may appear to be well mixed at first, but in time, they will always separate.

Chalk dust mixed with water forms a suspension.

Example Salt water is an example of a solution. Italian salad dressing is an example of a suspension.

Apply Prepare a cup of hot chocolate in a glass beaker. (Follow the directions on the package.) Observe the mixture for several minutes. Is the hot chocolate mixture a solution or a suspension? Explain.

_____

_____

_____

✓ Check Yourself

Matching

1. _____ acid
2. _____ carbon monoxide
3. _____ physical change
4. _____ chemical equation
5. _____ exothermic reaction

a. wood burning
b. $C + O_2 \rightarrow CO_2$
c. orange juice measures 4 on the pH scale
d. rock breaking
e. a colorless, odorless, toxic gas

Fill in the Blanks

suspension	solute	homogeneous mixture	dissolved	chemical formula

6. Brewed coffee is an example of a _____ _____.
7. When a substance has totally mixed with a liquid, it has _____.
8. Sugar, a substance that dissolves in a sugar water solution, is the _____.
9. Italian salad dressing is an example of a _____.
10. NaCl is the _____ _____ used to represent the compound sodium chloride.

Force and Motion

balanced forces / unbalanced forces

Confused Thinking The words balanced forces (**ba**-lənst **fôrs**-əz) and unbalanced forces (un-**ba**-lənst **fôrs**-əz) are confusing because the relationship between force and motion is not understood.

Straight Talk Force is a push or a pull. Force appears in pairs and can be either balanced or unbalanced. **Balanced forces** produce **no change** in the motion of an object. They are equal in size and opposite in direction. **Unbalanced forces** produce a **change** in the motion of an object in the direction of the greatest force.

Example

When the forces are balanced in a game of tug of war, the flag in the center of the rope will not move.

When the forces are unbalanced, the flag will move in the direction of the greatest force.

Apply Classify the examples as balanced or unbalanced forces. Record the answers in the data table.

Example	Force
1. a car being towed	
2. a person pushing on a cement wall	

centrifugal force / centripetal force

Confused Thinking The words centrifugal (sen-**tri**-fyə-gəl) force and centripetal (sen-**tri**-pə-təl) force are often confused because they have similar pronunciations and spellings, and the forces that control circular motion are not understood.

> **Word Clue**
> **Centripetal** is from Latin and means **"toward the center."**
> **Centrifugal** is also from Latin, and it means **"flee from the center."**

Straight Talk Both forces are important in describing circular motion. **Centrifugal force** causes objects to move **away** from the center. **Centripetal force** causes object to move in a circular path **toward** the center.

Example The outward movement felt as a car turns a sharp corner is an example of centrifugal force. The planets orbiting the sun are an example of centripetal force.

Apply Complete the data table below. Classify each example as a centripetal force or centrifugal force.

Example	Type of Force
1. moon orbiting Earth	
2. a person riding a merry-go-round	

Force and Motion

Newton's Laws of Motion

Confused Thinking Newton's Laws of Motion (**nōōt**-ns **lôz** uv **mō**-shən) are confusing because the laws are complicated and difficult to understand.

Straight Talk **Motion** is the act of **moving from one place to another**. Isaac Newton is the English scientist who stated the three laws of motion in 1687. The laws were named after him. **Newton's Laws of Motion** explain force, motion, acceleration, and mass.

Example
Newton's First Law of Motion: An object at rest tends to stay at rest, and an object in motion keeps moving in a straight line until an outside force stops it. (If a ball is not moving, it will stay that way until some force makes it move.)
Newton's Second Law of Motion: Acceleration depends on the mass of an object and the force pushing or pulling the object. (If two bike riders pedal with the same force, the rider moving less mass accelerates faster.)
Newton's Third Law of Motion: For every action, there is an equal and opposite reaction. (A boy jumps on a trampoline. The action is the boy pushing down on the trampoline. The reaction is the trampoline pushing up on the boy.)

Apply Complete the data table below. Record an example for each law.

Newton's Laws	Example
1. First Law of Motion	
2. Second Law of Motion	
3. Third Law of Motion	

simple machine / compound machine

Confused Thinking The words simple machine (**sim**-pəl mə-**shēn**) and compound machine (**kom**-pound mə-**shēn**) are confusing because the relationship between the two types of machines is not understood.

Straight Talk A **simple machine** does work with **one movement**. A **compound machine** is made from **two or more simple machines**.

Example The inclined plane, wedge, screw, lever, wheel and axle, and pulley are the six kinds of simple machines. A bicycle is an example of a compound machine. It is made from simple machines.

Apply Complete the data table below. Classify each example as a simple machine or compound machine.

Example	Type of Machine
1. scissors	
2. wheelchair ramp	
3. wheelbarrow	
4. a nail	

Force and Motion

speed / acceleration / velocity

Confused Thinking The words speed (**spēd**), acceleration (ak-sel-ə-**rā**-shən), and velocity (və-**lä**-sə-tē), are confusing because the relationships among the three terms are not understood.

Straight Talk **Speed** is the **distance** an object travels in a certain amount of **time. Acceleration** is any **change** in **speed or direction** of an object. **Velocity** is both the **speed** and **direction** that an object is moving.

Example A car travels on the highway. The speed of the car is 45 kilometers per hour. The velocity of the car is 45 kilometers per hour (speed) east (direction). The motion of the car is accelerated when the driver increases the speed to 55 kilometers per hour. The motion is accelerated again when the driver leaves the highway, changing the direction the car is traveling and decreasing the speed of the car.

Apply Complete the data table below. Classify each example of motion as speed, velocity, or acceleration.

Example	Describe Motion
1. An airplane is traveling 300 kp/h in a northeast direction.	
2. The long distance jogger's time was 6 mph for the race.	
3. A softball is hit into the outfield.	

✔ Check Yourself

Matching

1. _____ acceleration
2. _____ centripetal
3. _____ compound machine
4. _____ velocity
5. _____ balanced force

a. speed and direction that an object is moving
b. made from two or more simple machines
c. towards the center
d. produces no change in the motion of an object
e. change in speed or direction

Fill in the Blanks

compound machine	Third	First	acceleration	simple machine

6. A rocket being launched is an example of Newton's _____ Law of Motion.
7. A car stopped at a traffic light is an example of Newton's _____ Law of Motion.
8. A pulley is an example of a(n)_____ _____.
9. A fishing rod and reel is an example of a(n) _____ _____.
10. _____ occurs when the speed and direction of a race car changes.

Energy

conduction / convection / radiation

Confused Thinking The words conduction (kən-**duk**-shən), convection (kən-**vek**-shən), and radiation (rā-dē-**ā**-shən) are confusing terms because how they each transfer energy is not clearly understood.

Straight Talk Heat (thermal energy) always moves from warmer things to cooler things. Heat can be transferred in three ways: conduction, convection, and radiation. **Conduction** is the direct transfer of heat between **objects that touch. Convection** is the transfer of heat by the **movement of fluids** (like water and air) through currents. **Radiation,** or electromagnetic waves, can transmit heat **through a vacuum**. This energy comes in different wavelengths: radio, microwaves, infrared, visible light, ultraviolet light, x-rays, and gamma rays.

Example Stirring a bowl of hot soup with a spoon makes the spoon heat up; this is an example of conduction. When water boils in a pot, heat is transferred by convection. The sun heats Earth through the process of radiation.

Apply Complete the data table below. Classify the method used to transfer heat as conduction, convection, or radiation.

Example	Method of Transfer
1. rattlesnakes use infrared sensors to find prey in the dark	
2. hot air balloon rising into the air	
3. touching a hot pan from the oven	

heat / temperature

Confused Thinking The words heat (**hēt**) and temperature (**tem**-pər-ə-cho͞or) are confusing because the two terms are closely related in daily life, but in science, they have specific meanings.

Straight Talk In science, heat and temperature are not the same thing. **Heat** is the **transfer of energy** from one object to another. **Temperature** is a **measurement**. Heat and temperature are related; increasing or decreasing the heat changes the temperature.

Example When enough heat is added to water, the temperature rises. The temperature of the water can be measured with a thermometer. Temperature scales used on thermometers may be Fahrenheit, Celsius, or Kelvin scales.

Apply Complete the data table below. Measure and record the temperature of the water.

Water	Temperature	
	Fahrenheit (°F)	*Celsius (°C)*
1. tap water		
2. ice water (decrease heat)		
3. hot water (increase heat)		

Energy

kinetic energy / potential energy

Confused Thinking The words kinetic energy (ki-**net**-ik en-ər-jē) and potential energy (pə-**ten**-shəl en-ər-jē) are confusing because it is often difficult to tell the difference between the two types of energy.

Straight Talk There are two kinds of mechanical energy: kinetic and potential. **Kinetic energy** is the **energy of motion**. The amount of kinetic energy an object has depends on its mass and speed. **Potential energy** is **stored energy** that can be used to do work. The amount of stored energy depends on the object's position. Potential energy becomes kinetic energy when something acts to release the stored energy in the object.

Example A roller coaster car at the top of the hill has potential energy because even though it is not moving, it has the potential for movement because of its position. When it starts down the hill, the potential energy becomes kinetic energy. The higher the hill, the greater the potential energy of the roller coaster.

Apply Complete the data table. Classify each example as kinetic or potential energy.

Example	Energy
1. a ball bouncing	
2. a rocket on a launch pad	

mechanical waves / electromagnetic waves

Confused Thinking The words mechanical wave (mi-**kan**-ī-kəl wāv) and electromagnetic wave (i-lek-trō-**mag**-net-ik wāv) are confusing because the concepts are difficult to understand and picture.

Straight Talk A **mechanical wave** is a wave that cannot move its energy through a vacuum (empty space). Mechanical waves **require a medium**, such as liquid or gas, in order to move energy from one location to another. An **electromagnetic wave** is a wave that can move electrical and magnetic energy through a **vacuum**.

> *Amazing Fact*
> *Sound, a mechanical wave,* cannot be heard in outer space because there is no air in outer space.

Example Sound is a mechanical wave and can travel through air, solids, liquids, and gases. Light is an electromagnetic wave. Light from the sun reaches Earth through space (a vacuum).

Apply Complete the data table. Classify each example as a mechanical wave or an electromagnetic wave.

Example	Type of Wave
1. ocean waves	
2. ultraviolet waves	
3. radio waves	
4. earthquake waves	

Energy

work / power

Confused Thinking The words work (**wûrk**) and power (**pou**-ər) are confusing because they have several different meanings in everyday language, but in science, they have specific meanings.

Straight Talk **Work** occurs when a **force is applied** to an object, and the **object moves** as a result of the force. **Power** is the **measure** of how much **work is done** within a given **length of time**.

Example A boy lifting two boxes of the same shape and size off the floor and placing them on a shelf is an example of work. If it took the boy one minute to lift the first box and two minutes to lift the second box, the boy used more power to lift the first box.

Apply Complete the data table below. Classify each activity as an example of work or power.

Activity	Work or Power?
1. A sprinter runs the 50-yard dash.	
2. It took a weight-lifter five seconds to lift 500 pounds four feet.	
3. A truck tows a two-ton car two miles to a repair shop in 15 minutes.	
4. A player kicked the soccer ball down the center of the field.	

✓ Check Yourself

Matching
1. _____ conduction
2. _____ kinetic energy
3. _____ temperature
4. _____ mechanical wave
5. _____ power

a. the measure of how much work is done
b. measured with a thermometer
c. requires a medium in order to move energy
d. direct transfer of heat between objects that touch
e. energy of motion

Fill in the Blanks

x-ray	work	potential	convection	mechanical

6. A wave made by a slinky is an example of a _____ wave.
7. A flashlight battery is an example of _____ energy.
8. Pushing a box across the floor is an example _____.
9. Air currents are a result of the transfer of energy through the process of _____.
10. A(n) _____ is an electromagnetic wave.

Waves, Sound, and Light

absorption / transmission

Confused Thinking The words absorption (əb-**sôrp**-shən) and transmission (trans-**mish**-ən) are confusing because they are unfamiliar three-syllable words.

Straight Talk When matter **captures** light, it is called **absorption**. When light **passes through** matter, it is called **transmission**.

Example We see a red shirt because only red light is reflected off the shirt; all other colors of the spectrum that make up white light are absorbed. Light passing through a window is an example of transmission.

Apply Identify each picture as an example of the absorption or transmission of light.

sunlight through a window   a black cat

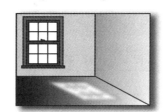

1. _____   2. _____

amplitude / loudness

Confused Thinking The words amplitude (**am**-pli-to͞od) and loudness (**loud**-nes) are confusing because the way energy is transported by waves is not understood.

Straight Talk One way energy is transported is through waves. A wave is the direction and speed energy travels in a back-and-forth or up-and-down motion. **Amplitude** is the distance a wave moves (the maximum **height of a wave crest or depth of a trough**) from its resting position. **Loudness** (volume) is the **human perception** of how much **energy** a sound wave carries. Volume is measured in decibels.

Example The larger the **amplitude**, the more energy carried by the wave. A volume knob controls the **loudness** of a radio.

Apply What is the amplitude of the wave? _____

Explain your answer.

_____
_____
_____
_____
_____

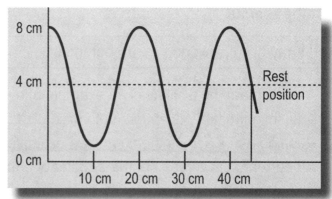

Waves, Sound, and Light

concave lens / convex lens

Confused Thinking The words concave lens (kon-**kāv lenz**) and convex lens (kon-**veks lenz**) are often confused because they have similar pronunciations and spellings, and they are unfamiliar opposites.

Straight Talk There are two types of lenses: concave and convex. A **concave** lens is thin in the middle and thicker on the edges, and light diffuses, or **spreads**, when it passes through the lens. A **convex** lens is thicker in the middle and thinner on the edges, and light converges, or **comes together**, when it passes through the lens.

> **Memory Trick**
> A **concave lens** curves inward like the opening to a cave.

Example Concave lenses shrink things. Convex lenses magnify. A good example of this is to take a spoon and look at your reflection. Looking at the concave side of the spoon (the front) will make you look smaller; looking at the convex side of the spoon (the back) will make you look bigger.

Apply Identify the type of lens pictured in each diagram.

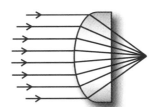
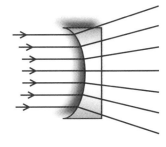

1. _____   2. _____

crest / trough

Confused Thinking The words crest (**krest**) and trough (**trof**) are easily confused because they are both used to describe parts of a wave.

Straight Talk The **highest point** of a wave is called the **crest**. The **lowest point** is called the **trough**.

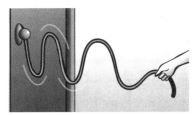

Example You can shake a rope attached to a doorknob, causing a wave motion. The rope moves up and down, creating high points and low points.

Apply Label the parts of the wave.

1. _____

2. _____

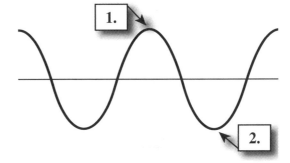

Waves, Sound, and Light

diffraction / interference

Confused Thinking The words diffraction (di-**frak**-shən) and interference (in-tər-**fîr**-əns) are often confused because the concepts are difficult to picture.

Straight Talk One way energy is transported is through waves. **Diffraction** is the **bending and spreading** of waves as they pass through or around a barrier. **Interference** occurs when **two waves meet** while traveling along the same medium.

Example When your mother shouts down the hallway, but you can still hear her in your room, that is one example of diffraction. When you look at a holographic sticker, the image is produced by interference.

Apply Identify the wave action as diffraction or interference.

1. _____   2. _____

frequency / pitch

Confused Thinking The words frequency (**frē**-kwən-sē) and pitch (**pich**) are confusing because the relationship between the two terms is not understood.

Straight Talk Sound travels in waves. A sound wave is a vibration that moves through matter. **Frequency** is the measurement of the **number of vibrations** an object makes. Frequency is measured in hertz (Hz); one hertz is equal to one wave per second. Objects that vibrate quickly have a high pitch; objects that vibrate more slowly have a low pitch. **Pitch** is the word used to describe how **high or low a sound is**. Pitch is what we hear.

Example A tuba vibrates slowly and produces a low pitch. A flute vibrates quickly and produces a high pitch.

Apply Place 5 empty glasses that are the same size in a line on a table. Fill one glass with water almost to the top. Fill the second glass about three-fourths full, the third half full, the fourth one-fourth full, and leave the last glass empty. Tap the side of each glass gently with a spoon.

Which glass has the highest pitch? _____ The lowest pitch? _____

Why? _____

Waves, Sound, and Light

longitudinal waves / transverse waves

Confused Thinking The words longitudinal wave (lon-jə-**tōōd**-nəl **wāv**) and transverse wave (**trans**-vûrs **wāv**) are confused because the way waves travel through a medium is not understood.

Straight Talk When a wave travels through matter, the particles of that medium (matter) vibrate. In a **longitudinal wave**, the motion of the particles is a **back-and forth** motion. In a **transverse wave**, the motion of the particles is an **up-and-down** motion.

Example Sound waves are longitudinal waves. Light waves are transverse waves.

Apply Identify the type of waves shown below.

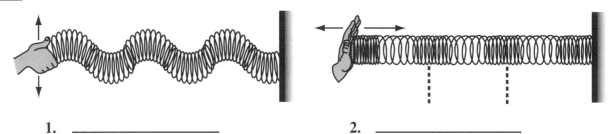

1. _____   2. _____

opaque / translucent / transparent

Confused Thinking The words opaque (ō-**pāk**), translucent (trans-**lōōs**-ənt), and transparent (trans-**par**-ənt) are often confused because the relationships among the three terms are not understood.

Straight Talk **Opaque** objects allow **no light** to pass through. You cannot see through opaque matter. **Translucent** objects allow **some light** to pass through. Objects on the other side of a translucent matter appear fuzzy and unclear. Objects that allow **all light** to pass through are called **transparent**. You can see through transparent matter.

> **Amazing Fact**
> *The glass catfish is almost totally **transparent**.*

Example A book is opaque. Waxed paper is translucent. Water is transparent.

Apply Complete the data table below. Classify each type of matter as transparent, translucent, or opaque.

Type of Matter	Transparent, Translucent, or Opaque?
1. metal	
2. tissue paper	
3. air	
4. plastic food wrap	

Waves, Sound, and Light

reflection / refraction

Confused Thinking The words reflection (ri-**flek**-shən) and refraction (ri-**frak**-shən) are often confused because they both deal with the behavior of light when it strikes an object.

Straight Talk **Reflection** is the light energy **bouncing** off an object or surface. **Refraction** is light energy **bending** as it moves from one medium into another medium.

Example You can see yourself in a mirror because of the reflection of light from the smooth surface of the mirror. Refraction explains why stars appear to twinkle. The light is traveling through the different mediums of space and Earth's atmosphere.

Apply Identify the pictures shown below as examples of reflection or refraction.

1. _____   2. _____   3. _____   4. _____

 Check Yourself

Matching

1. _____ opaque	a. number of vibrations per second
2. _____ interference	b. highest point of a wave
3. _____ transverse wave	c. up-and-down motion
4. _____ frequency	d. no light passes through the object
5. _____ crest	e. two waves meet

Fill in the Blanks

convex	transparent	transmission	trough	amplitude

6. Light shining into a room through a window is an example of _____.

7. To find the _____ of a wave, measure the height of a wave from its resting point.

8. A magnifying glass is an example of a(n) _____ lens.

9. The lowest point of a wave is called the _____.

10. Air is an example of matter that is _____.

Electricity and Magnetism

alternating current / direct current

Confused Thinking The words alternating current (ôl-tər-nāt-ing **kər**-ənt) and direct current (də-**rekt** kər-ənt) are easily confused due to the fact that electricity deals with invisible forces.

Straight Talk Current electricity is the continuous flow of electric charges. There are two kinds of current. **Alternating current** (AC) flows in one direction, then the direction **reverses**, or alternates. The flow of the current changes directions 60 times per second. **Direct current** (DC) is the flow of electricity in a circuit that moves in only **one** direction.

Example Electric companies provide homes and businesses with alternating current. Flashlight batteries produce direct current.

Apply Identify the type of current represented in each picture.

RELIABLE CAR BATTERY

1. _____   2. _____

attraction / repulsion

Confused Thinking The words attraction (ə-**trak**-shən) and repulsion (ri-**pəl**-shən) are confusing because they are terms used to explain both electricity and magnetism.

Straight Talk **Attraction** means to **move closer** together, and **repulsion** means to **move away** from. All matter is made of atoms that contain negative (electron) and positive (proton) charges. Two things with opposite, or different charges (a positive and a negative) will attract, or pull towards each other. Things with the same charge (two positives or two negatives) will repel, or push away from each other. The attraction and repulsion between charges causes both electric and magnetic forces.

Example The attraction between electrons and protons causes static electricity. The attraction or repulsion between the negative (North) and positive (South) poles of magnets is called magnetic force.

Apply Use the words *repel* and *attract* to answer the questions below.

1. Two positive electrical charges _____ each other.

2. A negative and a positive electrical charge _____ each other.

3. Like poles of magnets _____ each other.

4. Unlike poles of magnets _____ each other.

Electricity and Magnetism

conductor / insulator

Confused Thinking The words conductor (kən-**duk**-tər) and insulator (**in**-sə-lā-tər) are confusing because they are unfamiliar scientific opposites.

Straight Talk A **conductor** is a material that **will carry (conduct) electric current**. An **insulator** is a material that **does not conduct electricity**.

> **Amazing Fact**
> *Gold is one of the best* ***conductors*** *of electricity.*

Example Some metals are conductors of electricity. Shorter, thicker wires are better conductors than longer, thinner wires. Rubber, glass, plastic, and wood are examples of insulators.

Apply Complete the data table. Classify each object as a conductor or insulator.

Object	Conductor or Insulator?
1. plastic	
2. copper	
3. glass	
4. paper	
5. house key	
6. paper clip	

electric circuit / electric current

Confused Thinking The words electric circuit (i-**lek**-trik **sûr**-kət) and electric current (i-**lek**-trik kər-ənt) are often confused because they sound alike and there is not a clear understanding of a complete circuit.

Straight Talk An **electric circuit** is a continuous **path of flowing electrons** from a source, through wires and appliances, and back to the source. An **electric current** is the **flow** of electricity through wires. Electric currents are measured in amperes (amps).

> **Word Clue**
> ***Circuit*** *is related to the root word* ***circle****. A circle is represented by a closed figure; the circuit represents a continuous path through which electricity flows.*

Example An electric circuit is a closed or complete path. The SI unit of measurement for the rate of flow of electric current is the ampere or amp (A).

Apply Identify the pictures as relating to electric circuit or electric current.

1. _____   2. _____

Electricity and Magnetism

electricity / magnetism

Confused Thinking The words electricity (i-lek-**tris**-ət-ē) and magnetism (**mag**-nə-tiz-əm) are confusing because although these are different topics, there is a connection between them.

Straight Talk Electricity and magnetism are closely related. The movement of electrons causes both. **Electricity** comes from the **flow of electrons** from one atom to another. **Magnetism** is the **alignment of the electrons** in the same direction, creating a magnetic field. Every electric current has its own magnetic field. This magnetic force can be used to make an electromagnet.

Example Electricity is the flow of electrons. Magnetism is the alignment of electrons.

   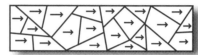

Apply Remove a few centimeters of insulation from each end of a one-meter-long insulated copper wire. Wrap the wire tightly around a large iron nail 20 times. Leave enough of the wire unwound so that you can attach it to the battery. Connect each end of the wire to a 6-volt battery.

How many paper clips can you pick up with the nail? _____

What can you infer about the relationship of electricity to magnetism? _____
_____

magnetic field / magnetic force

Confused Thinking The words magnetic field (mag-**net**-ik fēld) and magnetic force (mag-**net**-ik fōrs) are confusing because the difference between the two is not understood.

Straight Talk **Magnetic force** is an attractive or repulsive **force between the poles of magnets**. A **magnetic field** is the **space around a magnet** where there is a magnetic force.

Example   magnetic field   magnetic force

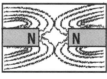    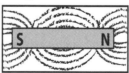

Apply Place a bar magnet in a plastic sandwich bag, and lay it on a table. Place a sheet of white paper on top of the bag. Sprinkle iron filings over the paper. The filings form a pattern that represents the magnetic field of the magnet. Draw the pattern below.

Electricity and Magnetism

series circuit / parallel circuit

Confused Thinking The words series circuit (**sîr**-ēz **sûr**-kit) and parallel circuit (**par**-ə-lel **sûr**-kit) are confusing because the difference between the two circuits is not understood.

Straight Talk A **series circuit** has **a single path** for electric current to flow. A **parallel circuit** has **more than one path** for electric current to flow.

Example Christmas lights used to be wired as a series circuit. If one light burned out, it caused a break in the circuit. There was no path for the current to take, so the other lights went out as well. Homes and businesses are wired using parallel circuits.

Apply Identify the type of circuit shown in each picture.

1. _____

2. _____

 Check Yourself

Matching

1. _____ alternating current
2. _____ electric current
3. _____ repulsion
4. _____ magnetism
5. _____ insulator

a. the flow of electricity through wires
b. alignment of the electrons
c. electricity flows in one direction, then reverses direction
d. does not conduct electricity
e. to move away from

Fill in the Blanks

amps	conductor	attract	parallel	direct

6. In a(n) _____ circuit, if one light burns out, the other lights will not be affected.

7. Electrical current is measured in _____.

8. Copper is a good _____ of electricity.

9. A flashlight is operated using _____ current power.

10. The unlike poles of a magnet _____ each other.

Structure of Life

cell cycle / cytokinesis

Confused Thinking The words cell cycle (**sel sī**-kəl) and cytokinesis (sī-tō-kə-**nē**-səs) are confusing because the process of cell division is not understood.

Straight Talk The **cell cycle** is the process of **cell division**: interphase, prophase, metaphase, anaphase, and telophase.

Interphase	Prophase	Metaphase	Anaphase	Telophase

Cytokinesis occurs during the telophase of the cell cycle. The **cytoplasm divides and one cell becomes two individual cells**.

Example Both animal and plant cells have a cell cycle. Cytokinesis in animals is where the cell pinches apart in the middle to form two new cells. In plants, a new cell wall forms between the two new cells during cytokinesis.

Apply Explain how cell cycle and cytokinesis are related. _____
_____

cell wall / cell membrane

Confused Thinking The words cell wall (**sel wôl**) and cell membrane (**sel mem**-brān) are confusing because they are invisible to the naked eye (microscopic) and they are both types of layers of a cell with different functions.

Straight Talk A **cell wall** is a **stiff protective layer** that surrounds the cell membrane in plants. The **cell membrane** is a **thin layer** that encloses the cell and **controls what enters and leaves** the cell of plants and animals.

Example

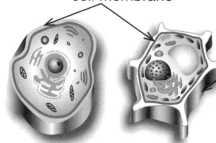

cell membrane

cell wall

animal cell   plant cell   Onion Cell

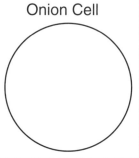

Apply With a needle, peel the thin clear tissue from the inside section of an onion. Carefully place the tissue flat on a slide. Smooth out any wrinkles in the tissue. Add a drop of iodine to the tissue. View the onion tissue under the microscope, and record your observations in the circle.

Structure of Life

diffusion / osmosis

Confused Thinking The words diffusion (dif-**yōō**-zhən) and osmosis (oz-**mō**-sis) are confusing because the relationship between the two terms is not fully understood.

Straight Talk The cell's membrane controls what enters and leaves a cell. To carry on life processes, oxygen, food, and water must pass into the cell and waste products must be removed from the cell through the membrane. The membrane has tiny holes in it. Molecules (very small substances) can go in and out of the cell by moving through the tiny holes. **Diffusion** is the movement of molecules into and out of the cell. **Example**

Osmosis is a special type of diffusion. **Osmosis** is the process that allows **water molecules** to move into and out of a cell.

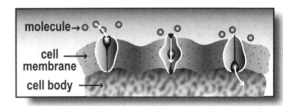

Apply Select an assortment of balloons and liquid food flavoring: vanilla, maple, banana, or coconut. Using a funnel, add a couple of drops of one flavoring to a balloon. Blow up the balloon and tie the end. Complete the procedure for each of the other food flavorings. After several minutes, smell the balloons.

Compare the activity to diffusion that occurs in cells. _____

_____

eukaryotic cell / prokaryotic cell

Confused Thinking The words eukaryotic cell (yōō-kar-ē-**ot**-ik **sel**) and prokaryotic cell (prō-kar-ē-**ot**-ik **sel**) are confusing because they have similar pronunciations and spellings, and the difference between the two types of cells is not understood.

Straight Talk There are two main types of cells. A **eukaryotic cell** is a single cell with a **nucleus**. A **prokaryotic cell** is the simplest type of cell. The cell has **no nucleus,** and DNA and other materials float freely inside the cytoplasm.

Eukaryotic	Prokaryotic
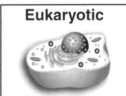	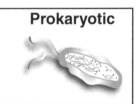

Example All organisms except bacteria are made up of eukaryotic cells. Bacteria are prokaryotic cells.

Apply Complete the data table below. Classify each cell as eukaryotic or prokaryotic.

Cell	Eukaryotic or Prokaryotic?
1. plant	
2. salmonella	
3. bacteria	
4. animal	

Structure of Life

multicellular / unicellular

Confused Thinking The words multicellular (muL-ti-**sel**-yə-lər) and unicellular (yo͞o-ni-**sel**-yə-lər) are confusing because they have similar pronunciations and spellings.

Straight Talk All organisms are made up of cells. **Multicellular** organisms are made up of **many cells**. **Unicellular** organisms are made up of **only one cell**.

Example Snails, fish, trees, and humans are all examples of multicellular organisms. Many organisms, including bacteria, are unicellular.

Apply Use the Venn diagram below to compare multicellular and unicellular organisms.

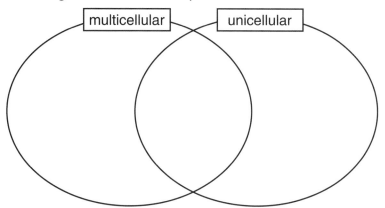

 Check Yourself

Matching

1. _____ eukaryotic cell
2. _____ cell membrane
3. _____ cytokinesis
4. _____ diffusion
5. _____ prokaryotic cell

   a. a cell that does not have a nucleus
   b. a single cell with a nucleus
   c. one cell becomes two individual cells
   d. movement of molecules into and out of the cell
   e. controls what enters and leaves the cell

Fill in the Blanks

telophase	plant	diffusion	prokaryotic	multicellular

6. Cytokinesis occurs during the _____ of the cell cycle.

7. A _____ cell has a cell wall surrounding the cell membrane.

8. Osmosis is a special type of _____.

9. Bacteria are a good example of _____ cells.

10. A cat is an example of a _____ organism.

Classification

amphibian / reptile

Confused Thinking The words amphibian (am-**fib**-ē-ən) and reptile (**rep**-tīl) are confusing terms because the characteristics of each animal group are not clear.

Straight Talk Vertebrates (animals with backbones) are divided into five groups. Each group has its own unique characteristics. Amphibians and reptiles are classified as vertebrates. The characteristics of each are shown in the chart.

Example

Vertebrates	Characteristics	Example
Amphibians	- most young have gills - most adults have lungs - lay eggs in water or moist ground - cold-blooded	Fire Newt
Reptiles	- dry, scaly skin - eggs have tough skin - cold-blooded	Rattlesnake

> ***Amazing Fact***
> *An **amphibian**, a frog breathes through its skin underwater; it also drinks through its skin.*

Apply Identify the vertebrates shown as amphibian or reptile.

1. _____   2. _____

angiosperm / gymnosperm

Confused Thinking The words angiosperm (**an**-jē-ə-spûrm) and gymnosperm (**jim**-nə-spûrm) are often confused because the difference between the two plant groups is not understood.

Straight Talk Angiosperms and gymnosperms are both members of the Plant Kingdom. **Angiosperms** are **flowering plants** that produce their seeds in fruit. Flowering plants are the most abundant type of plants on Earth. **Gymnosperms** are **nonflowering plants**, and the seeds are formed on a cone.

> ***Memory Trick***
> ***Angiosperm*** *means "covered seed."*
> ***Gymnosperm*** *means "bare seed."*

Example A tulip is an example of an angiosperm. A pine tree is an example of a gymnosperm.

Apply Divide a sheet of drawing paper in half. Label one half angiosperms and the other half gymnosperms. Using magazines and seed catalogs, cut out plant pictures and glue them under the correct heading on the paper.

Classification

autotroph / heterotroph

Confused Thinking The words autotroph (ô-tə-trōf) and heterotroph (**het**-ə-ro-trōf) are confusing because the concepts have been previously learned under different names.

Straight Talk Organisms can be classified by the way they get their food. An **autotroph** (producer) is an organism that **makes its own food** by using the Sun's energy. A **heterotroph** (consumer) is an organism that **gets energy from other organisms**.

Example In the food chain, an autotroph is a producer, and a heterotroph is a consumer.

Apply Complete the data table below. Classify each organism as an autotroph or heterotroph.

> **Word Clue**
> **auto** - a prefix meaning **self**
> **hetero** - a prefix meaning different; **other**
> **troph** - a suffix meaning **nourishment**; one who feeds

Organisms	Autotroph or Heterotroph?
1. cow	
2. tree	
3. algae	
4. fungi	

cold-blooded / warm-blooded

Confused Thinking The words cold-blooded (kōld-**blud**-id) and warm-blooded (**wôrm-blud**-id) are confusing because the difference between the two concepts is not understood.

Straight Talk **Cold-blooded** animals take on the temperature of their **surroundings**. **Warm-blooded** animals try to keep the inside of their bodies at a **constant** temperature.

> **Amazing Fact**
> As **cold-blooded** animals, crocodiles and alligators can go one year without eating.

Example All mammals and birds are warm-blooded. All reptiles, insects, arachnids, amphibians, and fish are cold-blooded.

Apply Identify the pictures shown below as warm-blooded or cold-blooded animals.

1. _____   2. _____   3. _____   4. _____

Classification

coniferous tree / deciduous tree

Confused Thinking The words coniferous tree (kō-**nif**-ər-əs **trē**) and deciduous tree (di-**sij**-oo-əs **trē**) are confusing because they have similar pronunciations and spellings. They are also closely related science terms.

Straight Talk Trees can be divided into two groups. **Coniferous** trees produce **seeds but not flowers**. The seeds are formed on cones. They usually have needle-like leaves that stay green throughout the year. **Deciduous** trees produce **seeds in flowers**. The green leaves stop making food in the fall and are **shed by the tree**. They are also known as broadleaf trees because the leaves are large and wide.

Example An oak tree is an example of a deciduous tree. Redwood trees, the tallest and one of the oldest trees in the world, are examples of coniferous trees.

Coniferous Trees	*Deciduous Trees*

Apply Make a folder book. Fold a sheet of construction paper vertically in half, like a hot dog bun. Unfold the paper. Fold the bottom edge of the paper up to form a two-inch packet and staple each side. Label one side of the folder "Coniferous Trees" and the other side "Deciduous Trees." Using magazines and seed catalogs, cut out pictures of trees and place them in the correct pocket of the folder.

dicot / monocot

Confused Thinking The words dicot (**dī**-kot) and monocot (**mon**-ə-kot) are confusing because both are classifications for flowering plants.

Straight Talk A **dicot** (dicotyledon) plant has **two cotyledons** in each seed, flowers with four or five petals, leaves with branching veins, and a taproot. A **monocot** (monocotyledon) plant has **one cotyledon** in each seed, flowers with petals of three or multiples of three, leaves with parallel veins, and fibrous roots.

Example

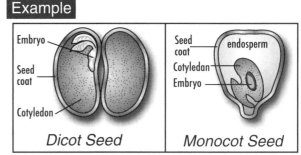

Dicot Seed   *Monocot Seed*

Apply Identify the pictures shown below as a dicot or monocot characteristic.

1. _____   2. _____   3. _____   4. _____

Classification

endoskeleton / exoskeleton

Confused Thinking The words endoskeleton (en-dō-**skel**-i-tən) and exo-skeleton (exō-**skel**-i-tən) are confusing because they have similar pronunciations and spellings. The idea of a skeleton is understood, but it is difficult to picture this structure being on the outside of an animal's body.

> **Word Clue**
> **endo** - a prefix meaning **inner**
> **exo** - a prefix meaning **outer**

Straight Talk All vertebrates have a **hard framework inside the body** that supports muscles and soft body parts called an **endoskeleton**. The endoskeleton grows as the body of the animal grows. Arthropods have a **hard outer skeleton** called an **exoskeleton**. It supports the weight of the animal. Once formed, an exoskeleton cannot get larger. But the arthropod inside keeps growing. When it gets too large for the exoskeleton, the exoskeleton splits. The arthropod sheds the old exoskeleton, and it grows a new one.

Example An elephant has an endoskeleton. A lobster has an exoskeleton.

Apply Complete the data table below. Classify the animals by their skeleton.

Organisms	Endoskeleton / Exoskeleton
1. snake	
2. spider	

gravitropism / phototropism / thigmotropism

Confused Thinking The words gravitropism (gra-**vi**-trə-pi-zəm), phototropism (fō-**tä**-trə-pi-zəm), and thigmotropism (thig-**mä**-trə-pi-zəm) are confusing because they have similar pronunciations and spellings, and the concept of tropism is not understood.

Straight Talk The growth of plants can be affected by changes in the environment. Tropism is plant growth in response to gravity, light, and touch. **Gravitropism** explains how **gravity** affects plant growth. **Phototropism** explains how **light** affects plant growth. **Thigmotropism** explains how **touch** affects plant growth.

Example Plant roots respond to gravity and grow down. Stems grow upward, or away from the pull of gravity. When a plant is placed near a window, the leaves will turn to face the light. Plants that vine will grow upward along a vertical support such as a fence.

Apply Identify the type of tropism shown in each illustration.

1. _____   2. _____   3. _____

Classification

innate behaviors / learned behaviors

Confused Thinking The words innate behaviors (i-**nāt** bē-**hā**-vyərs) and learned behaviors (**lûrnd** bē-**hā**-vyərs) are confusing because sometimes it is difficult to distinguish between the two behaviors.

Straight Talk **Innate behaviors** are instincts or traits that an animal is **born** with. They are passed through the genes from the parents to their young. **Learned behaviors** are **taught** to the animal, often by its parents.

Example Fish know how to swim immediately after being born; this is an example of an innate behavior. A dog sitting on cue from its owner is a learned behavior.

Apply Complete the data table below. Classify the behaviors as innate or learned.

Behavior	Innate or Learned?
1. a boy playing a piano	
2. a puppy chewing on a stick	
3. a bear hibernating	
4. a girl skateboarding	

phloem / xylem

Confused Thinking The words phloem (**flō**-em) and xylem (**zī**-ləm) are often confused because they are both names of tissue that are part of the plant's internal transportation system.

Straight Talk The stem transports water and food for the plant. Plants contain two basic types of tissue in the stem. **Phloem** is the tissue through which **food from the leaves moves down** through the rest of a plant. **Xylem** is the tissue through which **water and minerals move up** through a plant to the leaves.

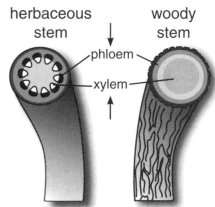

Example Use this trick to help remember which tissue does what. Phloem tissues help food flow down. Xylem tissues zip water up.

Apply Fill two glass beakers 3⁄4 full of water. Add several drops of red food coloring to the water. Cut one inch off the bottom end of a stalk of celery and discard. Place the celery stalk in the beaker of water. After 24 hours, cut off another inch piece from the bottom of the celery stalk. Use a magnifying glass to examine the cut. Cut the remaining celery stalk lengthwise and observe the structures. Which tissue, phloem or xylem, was involved in this experiment? _____

Classification

respiration / transpiration

Confused Thinking The words plant respiration (rĕs-pə-**rā**-shən) and transpiration (trăn-spi-**rā**-shən) are confusing because they have similar pronunciations and spellings, and how they are related to the process of photosynthesis is not understood.

Straight Talk **Respiration**, the **exchange of gases** between plants and the atmosphere, is a continuous cycle. The plant takes in carbon dioxide and gives off oxygen through the leaf during photosynthesis. Extra **water** the plant does not need for photosynthesis is **released** into the atmosphere through the leaf during **transpiration**.

Example

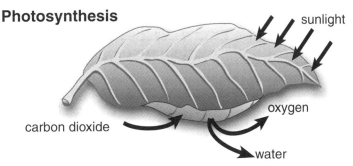

Photosynthesis

sunlight

carbon dioxide

oxygen

water

Apply On another sheet of paper, compare and contrast the process of respiration and transpiration using a Venn diagram.

vascular / nonvascular

Confused Thinking The words vascular (**vas**-kyə-lər) and nonvascular (non-**vas**-kyə-lər) are often confused because they have similar pronunciations and spellings.

Straight Talk **Vascular plants have tube-like structures** inside the plant used to carry food, water, and minerals. **Nonvascular plants do not have tube-like structures** to carry food and water throughout the plant.

> **Word Clue**
> ***non*** - a prefix meaning not

Example Vascular plants like tulips and oak trees have leaves, stems, and roots. Nonvascular plants like mosses and worts do not have stems or roots.

Apply Complete the data table at right. Classify the plants as vascular or nonvascular.

Plant	Vascular or Nonvascular?
1. moss	
2. walnut tree	
3. liverwort	
4. daisy	
5. celery	
6. green algae	

Classification

vertebrate / invertebrate

Confused Thinking The words vertebrate (**vûr**-tə-brāt) and invertebrate (in-**vûr**-tə-brāt) are often confused because they have similar pronunciations and spellings.

Straight Talk **Vertebrates** are animals that **have a backbone**. **Invertebrates** are animals that **do not have a backbone**.

> **Word Clue**
> *in* - a prefix meaning not

Example An earthworm is classified as an invertebrate because it does not have a backbone. A lizard is classified as a vertebrate because it has a backbone.

Apply Complete the data table below. Classify the animals as vertebrates or invertebrates.

Animal	Vertebrate or Invertebrate?
1. snake	
2. octopus	
3. frog	
4. leech	

✔ Check Yourself

Matching

1. _____ angiosperm
2. _____ heterotroph
3. _____ coniferous tree
4. _____ monocot
5. _____ warm-blooded animal

a. maintains a constant body temperature
b. plant that has one cotyledon in each seed
c. a flowering plant
d. gets energy from eating plants and animals
e. seeds are formed on cones

Fill in the Blanks

phloem	thigmotropism	transpiration	vertebrate	learned

6. A bean plant grabbing onto and growing upward along a fence is an example of

   _____.

7. An elephant performing in a circus is an example of _____ behavior.

8. Tissue that transports food from the leaves throughout the rest of a plant is the

   _____.

9. Water the plant does not need for photosynthesis is released during _____.

10. A turkey is classified as a _____ because it has a backbone.

Life Cycles

---

angiosperm / gymnosperm

Confused Thinking The words angiosperm (**an**-jē-ə-spûrm) and gymnosperm (**jim**-nə-spûrm) are confusing because the difference between flowering and nonflowering plants is not understood.

Straight Talk Angiosperms and gymnosperms are both members of the Plant Kingdom. **Angiosperms** are **flowering plants** that produce their **seeds in fruit. Gymnosperms** are **nonflowering plants**, and the seeds are formed on a **cone**.

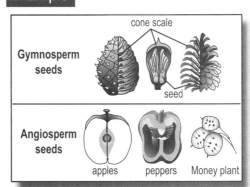
Example

Apply Pine tree seeds are found inside of the cones on the upper surface of each scale. Collect pine cones. Open pine cones have already dropped their seeds, so look for and collect cones that are still closed. Look on the ground around pine trees for ripe cones, sometime in the summer or early fall. After you collect the ripe cones, lay them out in the sun to dry. Once dry, the cones will open. Then place them in a paper bag and shake the cones to release the seeds. Examine the seeds and record your observations. _____

_____

---

asexual reproduction / sexual reproduction

Confused Thinking The words asexual reproduction (ā-**sek**-sho͞o-əl rē-prə-duk-shən) and sexual reproduction (**sek**-sho͞o-əl rē-prə-duk-shən) are confusing because the process of organisms making more of their own kind is not understood.

Straight Talk All living things reproduce, or make more of their own kind. **Asexual reproduction** occurs when a **single parent produces offspring** that are identical to the parent. **Sexual reproduction** occurs when **two parents combine a male cell and a female cell**, making a new organism that has traits from both parents in a process called fertilization.

Example Budding in plants is an example of asexual reproduction. Fish, horses, and humans reproduce by sexual reproduction.

Apply Complete the table by identifying the method of reproduction used by each plant as asexual or sexual.

	Plant	Method of Reproduction?
1.	tulip	
2.	pine tree	
3.	potato	
4.	strawberry plant	

Life Cycles

complete metamorphosis / incomplete metamorphosis

Confused Thinking The words complete metamorphosis (kəm-**plēt** met-ə-**môr**-fə-sis) and in-complete metamorphosis (in-kəm-**plēt** met-ə-**môr**-fə-sis) are confusing because they have similar pronunciations and spellings. They are also closely related science terms.

Straight Talk Animals reproduce to make more of their own kind. The stages in the life of an animal as it grows, develops, and matures vary for different kinds of organisms. **Complete meta-morphosis** is a life cycle including four stages: **egg, larva, pupa, and adult. Incomplete metamorphosis** is a life cycle with three stages: **egg, nymph, and adult**.

> **Word Clue**
> **meta** - a prefix meaning **change**
> **morph** - a base word from the Greek language meaning **shape**

Example Dragonflies go through the stages of incomplete metamorphosis. A butterfly goes through the stages of complete metamorphosis.

Apply Complete the data table below by identifying the life cycle of each animal as complete or incomplete metamorphosis.

Animal	Stages	Life Cycle
1. mosquito	egg / larva / pupa / adult	
2. dragonfly	egg / larva / adult	

larva / pupa

Confused Thinking The words larva (**lär**-və) and pupa (**pyü**-pə) are confusing because the stages of metamorphosis are not understood.

Straight Talk Complete metamorphosis in insects includes four stages: egg, larva, pupa, and adult. The **larva hatches from the egg**. It is different in appearance and behavior from a fully grown adult. During the **pupa** stage, an insect **transforms from the larva to an adult**. The insect is usually enclosed in a protective covering while it undergoes these changes.

Example

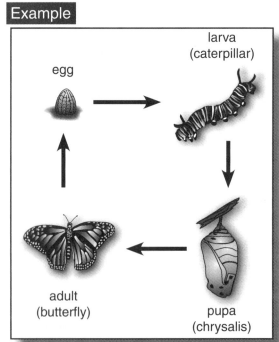

egg

larva (caterpillar)

pupa (chrysalis)

adult (butterfly)

Apply Answer the questions below.

1. In the life cycle of a butterfly, the larva is often called a(n) _____.

2. In the life cycle of a butterfly, the hard shell pupa is called a(n) _____.

Life Cycles

seed / spore

Confused Thinking The words seed (**sēd**) and spore (**spôr**) are confusing because it is a misconception that all plants are grown from seeds.

Straight Talk A **seed** is an **undeveloped plant with stored food** sealed in a protective covering. Seeds are produced by flowering plants. They are the product of sexual reproduction. A **spore** is usually a **single cell capable of growing into a new plant**. Spores are produced by nonflowering plants. Spores are an example of asexual reproduction.

Example Flowers and trees produce seeds. Mosses, lichens, and ferns are among the plants that produce spores.

Apply Ferns reproduce from spores, not flowers. On the underside of a fertile frond are clusters of brown dots. The dots are made up of many spore cases. Examine a fern frond with spore cases. Use a toothpick to open a spore case. Examine the spores with a magnifying glass. Record your observations. _____

_____

 Check Yourself

Matching

1. _____ angiosperm
2. _____ complete metamorphosis
3. _____ seed
4. _____ spore
5. _____ gymnosperm

a. an example of asexual reproduction
b. egg, caterpillar, chrysalis, butterfly
c. classification of flowering plants
d. the product of sexual reproduction
e. classification of nonflowering plants

Fill in the Blanks

spore	asexual	complete	angiosperm	caterpillar

6. A strawberry plant is an example of _____ reproduction.
7. A flowering plant that produces its seeds in fruit is called a(an) _____.
8. A single cell capable of growing into a new plant is called a(an) _____.
9. In the life cycle of a butterfly, the words larva or _____ can be used to describe the same stage.
10. A mosquito goes through the stages of _____ metamorphosis.

Reproduction and Heredity

dominant / recessive

Confused Thinking The words dominant (**dom**-ə-nənt) and recessive (ri-**ses**-iv) are confusing because the concept of heredity is not understood.

Straight Talk The characteristics of all living things are called traits. Every living thing is a collection of inherited traits (characteristics passed down to an individual by his or her parents). A trait may be **dominant** (**stronger**), and that trait will show up in the organism. If a trait is **recessive** (**weaker**), that trait will not show up in the organism unless the organism inherits two recessive genes for that trait.

Example A dominant gene gives people the ability to curl their tongue. Hair turning counterclockwise on the crown of your head is caused by a recessive gene.

Apply Your genes have been inherited from your parents. Below are two common traits controlled by genes. Do you have any of these traits? Do your parents? Record the answers in the data table below.

Traits [dominant (D) and recessive (r)]	You	Mother	Father
Dimples (D): natural smile produces dimples in one or both cheeks or a dimple in the center of the chin	Yes/No	Yes/No	Yes/No
Attached Earlobes (r): earlobes directly attached to head	Yes/No	Yes/No	Yes/No

gene / chromosome

Confused Thinking The words chromosome (**krō**-mə-sōm) and gene (**jēn**) are confusing because the concept of heredity is not understood.

Straight Talk By studying heredity, scientists learned how traits are passed from parents to their offspring. Traits are controlled by genes made up of DNA located on the chromosomes. **Chromosomes (rod-shaped strands) containing genetic material** are located in the nucleus of the cell. The chromosome is divided into many small sections. These sections are called genes. The **genes consist of a long strand of DNA**. The DNA contains the genetic blueprint for how an organism looks and functions (traits).

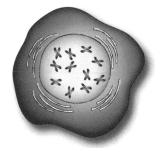

Example Humans have 23 pairs of chromosomes. The genes on the chromosomes carry the hereditary instructions for the cell.

Apply Explain the relationship between chromosomes and genes. _____

_____

Reproduction and Heredity

genotype / phenotype

Confused Thinking The words genotype (jē-nə-tīp) and phenotype (fē-nə-tīp) are confusing because they have similar pronunciations and spellings.

Straight Talk The **inherited combination** of genes is known as the offspring's **genotype**. An organism's **inherited appearance** is called its **phenotype**.

Apply The Punnett square shows the cross between two tall pea plants. Each one has one tall gene and one short gene. The genetic makeup of an organism is

Example

Punnett Square

A lowercase letter represents a recessive trait.

Father's Genes

	T	t
T	**TT** offspring tall	**Tt** offspring tall
t	**Tt** offspring tall	**tt** offspring short

Mother's Genes

A capital letter represents a dominant trait.

The square is filled in by writing one gene for each parent in each box.

the genotype. The genotype of the mother is Tt, and the genotype of the father is Tt. They each have a tall gene and a short gene, but because the tall gene is dominant, both plants' phenotype (appearance) is tall. What are the three possible genotypes for the offspring?

_____

The phenotype of 75 percent or 3⁄4 of the offspring will be _____.

identical twins / fraternal twins

Confused Thinking The words identical twins (ī-**den**-ti-kəl **twinz**) and fraternal twins (frə-**tər**-nəl **twinz**) are confusing because many people do not realize there is a difference in the two types of twins.

Straight Talk **Identical twins** develop when **one egg is fertilized by one sperm**, and then it splits into two different cells. **Fraternal twins** develop when **two separate eggs are fertilized by two different sperm** at the same time.

Example Identical twins have exactly the same genes. Therefore, they look alike, talk alike, and can even think alike. Because they have exactly the same genes, identical twins are either both girls or both boys. Fraternal twins' genetic connection is the same as siblings born at separate times. They may look alike, or they may not. This is why fraternal twins can be of the opposite sex.

Apply You meet a set of twins. They look alike, but one is a boy and the other is a girl. Are they identical twins or fraternal twins? _____ Explain. _____

_____

Reproduction and Heredity

mitosis / meiosis

Confused Thinking The words meiosis (mī-ō-sis) and mitosis (mī-tō-sis) are confusing because the words sound alike, and although the end results are different, the first five steps involved in each process are the same.

Straight Talk All living things grow and repair themselves by the process of **mitosis (cell division)**. The cell contents and the DNA are divided equally between two daughter cells (new cells). **Meiosis** is cell division that **forms reproductive cells** (eggs and sperm). These cells have only half the genetic material as a normal cell.

Example The first five phases of cell division are the same for both mitosis and meiosis. In meiosis, the new cells go through a second division of the nucleus in which four new cells (reproductive cells) with half the number of chromosomes are formed.

Mitosis					Meiosis
Interphase	**Prophase**	**Metaphase**	**Anaphase**	**Telophase**	Reproductive cells formed

Apply Fill in the Blanks

1. The process of mitosis produces cells for _____.

2. The process of meiosis produces _____.

✔ Check Yourself

Matching

1. _____ dominant
2. _____ phenotype
3. _____ identical twins
4. _____ mitosis
5. _____ genotype

a. the process of cell growth and repair
b. one egg is fertilized by one sperm, then it divides
c. stronger
d. inherited appearance
e. inherited combination of genes

Fill in the Blanks

chromosomes	DNA	identical	gene	reproductive

6. Because they have exactly the same genes, _____ twins are either both girls or both boys.

7. Traits are controlled by genes made up of DNA located on the _____.

8. A Punnett square predicts all possible _____ combinations for the offspring of two parents.

9. Meiosis only happens in the formation of _____ cells.

10. Genes consist of a long strand of _____.

Ecology

abiotic factor / biotic factor

Confused Thinking The words abiotic factor (ā-bī-**ot**-ik **fak**-tər) and biotic factor (bī-**ot**-ik **fak**-tər) are confusing because they have similar pronunciations and spellings, and the difference between the two terms is not understood.

Straight Talk An environment consists of two parts: abiotic factors and biotic factors. The **abiotic factors** include the **nonliving things** in the environment. The **biotic factors** include all the organisms **living** in the environment.

Example Water, soil, light, and temperature are considered abiotic factors in an ecosystem. Animals are examples of biotic factors in an ecosystem.

Apply Complete the data table. Classify each factor as abiotic or biotic.

Factor	Abiotic or Biotic?
1. algae	
2. pond water	
3. iceberg	
4. moss	

climax community / pioneer community

Confused Thinking The words climax community (**klī**-maks kə-**myōo**-ni-tē) and pioneer community (pī-ə-**nîr** kə-**myōo**-ni-tē) are confusing because the series of environmental changes in the ecological succession of a community is not understood.

Straight Talk Living communities change over time. Ecological succession (a series of environmental changes that occur in an ecosystem) are the result of the activities of man, other living things, or when natural disasters occur such as forest fires, floods, climate changes, or volcanic eruptions. These activities may reduce an area to bare soil or rock. The **first organisms to return to a disrupted area**, such as grasses, form a **pioneer community**. Eventually, animals return, and given a sufficient amount of time, new communities form. A **climax community** or **stable ecosystem** finally forms that may remain the same for many years.

Example In a newly formed volcanic island, the pioneer community is made up of bacteria, fungi, and algae. A forest is considered a climax community because it has reached the final stage of succession.

Apply In 1980, Mount St. Helens erupted, destroying a forest biome. Explain how the process of ecological succession will change the area back to a thriving forest once again.

_____

_____

_____

Ecology

commensalism / mutualism / parasitism

Confused Thinking The words commensalism (kə-**men**-sə-liz-əm), mutualism (**myoo**-choo-ə-liz-əm), and parasitism (**par**-ə-sī-tiz-əm), are confusing because the role symbiosis plays in maintaining the natural balance of an ecosystem is not understood.

Straight Talk Ecosystems are very delicate and must maintain a natural balance. Organisms maintain this natural balance through symbiosis (relationships between two organisms). There are three different types of symbiosis. **Commensalism** is a relationship between two kinds of organisms that **benefits one without harming the other**. **Mutualism** is a relationship between two kinds of organisms that **benefits both**. **Parasitism** is a relationship in which **one organism benefits** from that relationship while **the other organism may be harmed** by it.

Example The relationship between a Monarch butterfly and a milkweed plant is an example of commensalism. Flowers and their pollinators are a common form of mutualism. A tick attached to a dog is an example of parasitism.

Apply Mutualism can be seen between the wrasse (sometimes called the cleaner fish) and larger fish. The wrasse fish swims inside a large fish's mouth; the wrasse eats dead skin, parasites, lice, and other irritants. It also cleans the external parts of the larger fish. The larger fish relies on the cleaning activities of the wrasse to stay healthy. Explain how this is an example of mutualism. _____

_____

food chain / food web

Confused Thinking The words food chain (**food chān**) and food web (**food web**) are confusing because they are closely related science concepts explaining the flow of energy between organisms in an ecosystem.

Straight Talk Food chains and food webs are tools used to represent the flow of energy from one organism to another organism back to the sun. A **food chain** is a diagram of **who eats what**. A **food web** is a diagram of **two or more food chains** linked together.

Example When the cardinal eats the beetle that eats the plants, that's a food chain. But the cardinal also eats ants, butterflies, worms, and spiders, and those insects eat other plants and animals, forming their own food chains. All those food chains together make a food web.

Apply Answer the questions below.

1. What would probably happen if the cardinal was removed from the food web? _____

_____

2. What is the primary source of all energy in the food web? _____

Ecology

grassland / savanna

Confused Thinking The words grassland (**gras**-land) and savanna (sə-**van**-ə) are confusing because a savanna is a type of grassland.

Straight Talk Scientists have divided the world into biomes (areas having similar plants, animals, and climates). **Grassland is a biome dominated by grasses**. A **savanna** is a **type of grassland**.

Example A savanna has warm temperatures year round. There are two very different seasons in a savanna; a long, dry winter, and a wet summer. The vegetation consists of tall stiff grasses with clumps of trees. Savannas are found in Africa and in South America.

Apply Research grasslands. Use the information to complete the data table below.

Biome	Description	Examples of Plants	Examples of Animals
1. savanna			
2. steppe			
3. prairies			

habitat / niche

Confused Thinking The words habitat (**hab**-i-tat) and niche (**nich**) are confusing because they are closely related science terms.

Straight Talk Relationships in an ecosystem can be complex. Individuals within populations may compete trying to use the same limited resources: food, water, and space. Only those organisms able to get the resources they need will survive. Having a specific **habitat, where a plant or animal lives in the ecosystem**, and **niche, a special job a plant or animal does in the ecosystem**, allows an organism to reduce competition for the things it needs.

Amazing Fact
*1992's Hurricane Andrew damaged the protected **habitat** of the Florida tree snail. Florida Game and Freshwater Fish Commission has named the snail a Species of Concern. This designation protects them, dead or alive, from the collectors of their brightly colored spiraled shells.*

Example The dolphin lives in a marine habitat. The niche of the honeybee in the ecosystem is to carry pollen from one flower to the next.

Apply Complete the table below. Identify the habitat and the niche for each organism.

Organism	Habitat	Niche
1. earthworm		
2. vulture		
3. honeybee		
4. wrasse		

Ecology

herbivore / carnivore / omnivore

Confused Thinking The words herbivore (**hûr**-bə-vôr), carnivore (**kär**-nə-vôr), and omnivore (**om**-nə-vôr) are confusing because they are three-syllable words that have the same ending, and the difference between them is not clear.

Straight Talk All animals are consumers. Each animal has a diet that meets its individual needs for survival. When an animal eats other animals or plants, the stored energy in those organisms is passed along to the consumer. There are three kinds of consumers: herbivores, carnivores, and omnivores. A **herbivore** is an organism that gets energy from **eating plants** (leaves, flowers, fruits, or even wood). A **carnivore** is an organism that gets energy from **eating other animals**. An **omnivore** is an organism that gets energy from **eating plants and animals**.

Example A cow is classified as a herbivore. A lion is classified as a carnivore. Humans are omnivores because they eat both plants and animals.

Apply Complete the data table. Classify each animal as a herbivore, carnivore, or omnivore.

Animal	Herbivore / Carnivore / Omnivore
1. chicken	
2. eagle	
3. squirrel	

predator / prey

Confused Thinking The words predator (**pred**-ə-tər) and prey (**prā**) are often confused because the relationship between organisms in an ecosystem is not understood.

Straight Talk Organisms in an ecosystem have special feeding relationships. Animals that **kill and eat other animals** for energy are **predators**. Animals that **are killed and eaten** for their energy are called **prey**.

Example

Predator	→	Prey
lion	→	wildebeest
coyote	→	rabbit

> **Amazing Fact**
> *There is a cockroach in Madagascar that hisses to scare away **predators**.*

Apply Complete the data table below. List three predators and their prey.

Predator	Prey
1.	
2.	
3.	

Ecology

producer / consumer / decomposer

Confused Thinking The words producer (prǝ-**dōō**-sǝr), consumer (kǝn-**sōō**-mǝr), and decomposer (dē-kǝm-**pōz**-ǝr) are confusing because the exchange of energy in an ecosystem is not understood.

Straight Talk The food chain consists of three levels: producers, consumers, and decomposers. A **producer** is an organism that **changes the sun's energy into food**. A **consumer** is an organism that **gets energy from eating plants and other animals**. A **decomposer** is an organism that **gets energy from dead or decaying organisms**.

Example Plants are producers. All animals are consumers. A worm is a decomposer.

Apply Answer the questions below.

1. A beetle is an example of a _____.
2. Green algae is an example of a _____.
3. A mushroom is an example of a _____.

organism / population / community

Confused Thinking The words organism (**ôr**-gǝ-niz-ǝm), population (pop-yǝ-**lā**-shǝn), and community (kǝ-**myōō**-ni-tē) are confusing because the different levels of an ecosystem are not known.

Straight Talk An ecosystem is the interaction of all the living and nonliving things in an environment. Ecologists organize an ecosystem into three levels: organism, population, and community. An **organism** is a **living thing**. A **population** is **all the organisms of one species**. **Community** is the **living and nonliving things** in the ecosystem.

Example

An elk is a living organism.

It is a member of a population.

It lives in a forest community.

Apply Complete the graphic organizer. Write the definition for each level of an ecosystem.

Organism		Population		Community
	→		→	

Ecology

taiga / tundra

Confused Thinking The words taiga (tī-gə) and tundra (**tun**-drə) are confusing because both are unfamiliar biomes.

Straight Talk A **taiga** is a cool **forest biome of conifers** in the upper Northern Hemisphere. The **tundra** is the **treeless plain in arctic regions**, where the ground is frozen all year. The taiga begins where the tundra ends and consists of mainly fir and spruce trees.

Example

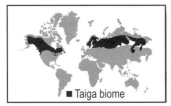

■ Taiga biome

The taiga biome stretches across a large portion of Canada, Europe, and Asia.

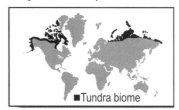

■ Tundra biome

The tundra biome, located south of the ice caps of the Arctic, extends across North America, Europe, and Siberia.

Apply Each biome has its own unique climate, plants, and animals. Research the two biomes and use the information to complete the data table below. Copy the table to your own paper if you need more space.

	Biome	Description	Examples of Plants	Examples of Animals
1.	taiga			
2.	tundra			

✓ Check Yourself

Matching

1. _____ abiotic factors
2. _____ pioneer community
3. _____ food chain
4. _____ savanna
5. _____ niche

a. a diagram of who eats what
b. the nonliving things in the environment
c. first organisms to return to a disrupted area
d. a special job a plant or animal does in the ecosystem
e. a type of grassland

Fill in the Blanks

population	consumers	bear	prey	taiga

6. A _____ is an omnivore because it eats both plants and animals.

7. A quail is a fox's _____.

8. All animals are _____.

9. A _____ is all the organisms of one species.

10. The _____ is a cool forest biome of conifers in the upper Northern Hemisphere.

Geology

---

chemical weathering / mechanical weathering

Confused Thinking The words chemical weathering (**kem**-i-kəl **we**th-ər-ing) and mechanical weathering (mi-**kan**-i-kəl **we**th-ər-ing) are confusing because both terms end with the word weathering.

Straight Talk Weathering changes the earth's surface over time. **Chemical weathering** is the **wearing away of rock by oxidation or dissolving by acid**. **Mechanical weathering** is the **physical forces such as wind, water, plants, and freezing that break rock into smaller pieces**.

Example Chemical weathering in caves causes stalactites and stalagmites. Mechanical weathering can be seen when expanding ice breaks a rock into smaller pieces.

Apply Identify each picture as an example of chemical or mechanical weathering.

1. _____   2. _____

---

continental drift / plate tectonics

Confused Thinking The words continental drift (kän-tə-**nən**-təl **drift**) and plate tectonics (**plāt** tek-**tä**-niks) are confusing because both terms are used to explain the present location of the continents.

Straight Talk **Continental drift** is the theory, proposed in the early 1900s, that a supercontinent called Pangaea broke apart, forming the seven continents. The **continents slowly drifted to their present positions**. Today, scientists use **plate tectonics** to explain how the continents were able to move to their present locations. Scientists believe the earth's outermost layer, the lithosphere, broke apart and formed seven large plates (pieces). The **motion of magma, just under the crust, causes the movement of the plates**.

Example Scientists believe the seven continents were once part of a supercontinent called Pangaea.

Apply Answer the questions below.
1. The movement of the earth's plates over millions of years is called _____.
2. How do scientists explain the movement of the continents to their present positions?

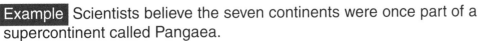

Geology

---

crust / mantle / core

Confused Thinking The words crust (**krəst**), mantle (**man**-təl), and core (**kȯr**) are confusing because the interior of the earth is not understood.

Straight Talk The earth has three layers: the crust, mantle, and core. The **crust** is a **thin rocky skin** covering the earth. The **mantle** is a **hot, plastic layer** of melted rock that surrounds the core of the earth. The **core** is the **center of the earth**. It is divided into an inner core and an outer core.

Example The crust is mostly solid. High temperatures form magma that flows in the mantle layer. The core is divided into two layers: a liquid outer core made up mostly of iron and nickel and a solid inner core composed of solid iron and nickel.

1. _____
2. _____
3. _____
4. _____

Apply Label the layers of the earth shown in the diagram at right.

---

crystal / mineral / rock

Confused Thinking The words crystal (**kris**-təl), mineral (**min**-ər-əl), and rock (**rok**) are confusing because they are closely related concepts.

Straight Talk The basic material that makes up the earth's crust is rock. All **rocks** are **made of minerals**. A **mineral** is a **solid material that occurs naturally in the earth's crust**. The **atoms of minerals are arranged in a certain pattern** and form **crystals**.

> **Amazing Fact**
> Iron is a **mineral** essential for life. It is found in every living cell and is important for the production of hemoglobin, an important ingredient of red blood cells.

Example Minerals are made of crystals. Crystals form in one of six distinct shapes.

cubic   hexagonal   monoclinic   orthorhombic   tetragonal   triclinic

Apply Examine the crystal shape of salt. Sprinkle salt on black paper. Examine the crystals with a magnifying glass. Compare the shape of the salt crystals to the six basic crystal shapes above. What is the shape of the salt crystals? _____

Geology

erosion / weathering

Confused Thinking The words erosion (i-**rō**-zhən) and weathering (we*th*-ər-ing) are confusing because both terms deal with actions that change the surface of the earth.

Straight Talk **Erosion** is the **wearing away of the earth's surface** by wind, water, ice, or gravity. Erosion takes away the soil in one place and deposits it in another. **Weathering** in this case is chemical weathering, which is the **wearing away of rock** by oxidation or dissolving by acid.

Example Planting trees and grasses slows erosion. Weathering in caves causes stalactites and stalagmites.

Apply Complete the data table. Classify each example as a result of erosion or weathering.

Example	Erosion or Weathering?
1. Grand Canyon	
2. Soil formation	
3. Mississippi Delta	
4. Carlsbad Caverns	
5. Features on the Great Sphinx disappearing	

extrusive igneous rocks / intrusive igneous rocks

Confused Thinking The words extrusive igneous (ik-**strü**-siv **ig**-nē-əs) rocks and intrusive igneous (in-**trü**-siv **ig**-nē-əs) rocks are confusing because both terms deal with the formation of rocks by volcanic action.

Straight Talk Magma that reaches the earth's surface is called lava. When **lava** cools, it forms **extrusive igneous rocks**. **Magma** that cools inside the earth forms **intrusive igneous rocks**.

> **Word Clue**
> *ex* - a prefix meaning **out**
> *in* - a prefix meaning **in**

Example   Basalt is an example of extrusive igneous rock.

Granite is an example of intrusive igneous rock.

Apply Fill in the blanks below.

1. When _____ cools, it forms extrusive igneous rocks.
2. When _____ cools inside the earth, it forms intrusive igneous rocks.

Geology

focus / epicenter

Confused Thinking The words focus (**fō**-kəs) and epicenter (**e**-pi-sen-tər) are confusing because earthquakes are not understood.

Straight Talk The earth's crust is broken up into large sections that move. When two sections meet, pressure builds up. When too much pressure builds up, the rocks suddenly slide past each other, and the pressure is released. The result is an earthquake. The **place in the earth's crust where the pressure was released** is called the **focus**. The focus can be many kilometers below in the crust. Earthquake waves spread out in all directions from the focus. The earthquake's **epicenter** is the spot on the earth's surface **directly above the focus**.

Example The epicenter of the 1906 San Francisco Earthquake occurred offshore about two miles from the city.

Apply Use the words focus, epicenter, and fault to label the diagram of an earthquake.

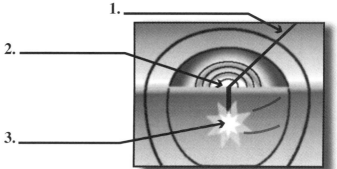

1. _____

2. _____

3. _____

folded mountain / faulted mountain

Confused Thinking The words folded mountain (**fōld**-id mount-n) and faulted mountain (**fôlt**-id mount-n) are confusing because the process of mountain building is not understood.

Straight Talk Movement in the earth's crust creates mountains. Mountains are classified by the way they are formed. **Folded mountains** are formed when the earth's crust **folds into great waves**. **Faulted mountains** are formed when the earth's crust **breaks into huge blocks**. Some blocks move upward and some move downward.

Example The Rocky Mountain Range was formed by the folding of the earth's curst. The Teton Mountain Range is an example of faulted mountains.

Apply Identify the type of mountains shown in the pictures as folded or faulted.

1. _____   2. _____

Geology

gem / ore

Confused Thinking The words gem (**jem**) and ore (**or**) are confusing because they are both minerals.

Straight Talk A mineral is a solid material that occurs naturally in the earth's crust. A **gem** is a **rare mineral that can be cut and polished**. An **ore** is a **mineral from which the metal can be removed**.

Example Diamonds and emeralds are rare gems. Many of the metals we use such as copper and nickel come from ores.

> **Amazing Fact**
> *A diamond is a rare **gem**. A diamond is the hardest known substance on the earth.*

Apply Complete the data table. Classify each mineral as a gem or a metal from an ore.

Mineral	Gem or Ore?
1. gold	
2. ruby	
3. iron	

igneous rock / sedimentary rock / metamorphic rock

Confused Thinking The words igneous rock (**ig**-nē-əs **rok**), metamorphic rock (met-ə-**môr**-fik **rok**), and sedimentary rock (sed-ə-**men**-tə-rē **rok**) are confusing because how rock is formed is not understood.

Straight Talk **Igneous rock**, known as fire rock, is the rock formed by the **cooling** of melted material such as **magma inside the earth and lava above ground**. **Sedimentary rock** is the rock formed from **sediments** (sand, clay, and other materials that settle in water). **Metamorphic rock** is the rock formed when sedimentary or igneous rocks **undergo a change due to pressure or heat in the earth**.

Example

Obsidian is igneous rock that forms when lava cools quickly above ground.	Sandstone is sedimentary rock formed when layers of sediment become solid.	Marble is metamorphic rock transformed from limestone into a new kind of rock.

Apply Unscramble the letters to find the correct terms.

1. CHPRMTEAOMI rocks have changed into another kind of rock. _____
2. SNGIEOU rock is known as fire rock. _____

Geology

lava / magma

Confused Thinking The words lava (**lä**-və) and magma (**mag**-mə) are confusing because they are both molten (melted) rock produced by the earth.

Straight Talk **Lava** is the molten rock that **emerges from a volcano**. **Magma** is the molten rock found **below the earth's crust**. Igneous rock, known as fire rock, is the rock formed by the cooling of melted material such as magma inside the earth and lava above ground.

Example Once exposed at the surface, magma becomes lava. Magma that flows from volcanoes is called lava.

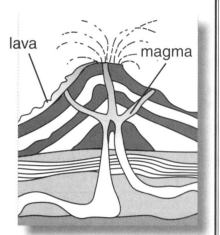

Apply Fill in the word-shaped boxes with letters to make the statement true.

Igneous rock, known as [   ][   ][   ][   ] rock, is formed by the cool-

ing of melted material, such as [   ][   ][   ][   ][   ] inside the earth

and [   ][   ][   ][   ] above ground.

 Check Yourself

Matching

1. _____ chemical weathering
2. _____ core
3. _____ erosion
4. _____ faulted mountains
5. _____ igneous rocks

a. taking away of the soil
b. fire rocks
c. center of the earth
d. wearing away of rock
e. the earth's crust breaks into huge blocks

Fill in the Blanks

ores	lava	focus	sedimentary	magma

6. Magma that flows from volcanoes is called _____.
7. When _____ cools inside the earth, it forms intrusive igneous rocks.
8. When layers of sediment become solid, _____ rocks are formed.
9. Many of the metals that we use come from _____.
10. The _____ of an earthquake can be many kilometers below, in the earth's crust.

Oceanography

continental shelf / continental slope / continental rise

Confused Thinking The words continental shelf (kän-tə-**nən**-təl **shelf**), continental slope (kän-tə-**nən**-təl **slōp**), and continental rise (kän-tə-**nən**-təl **rīz**) are confusing because it is not understood that the continents do not end at the shoreline.

Straight Talk The continents do not end at the shoreline. They continue under the sea to the deep ocean floor. The **continental shelf** is the **land near the shoreline that is covered with water**. At the end of the shelf, the **land plunges downward** sharply, forming the **continental slope**. At the bottom of the continental slope, **sediment that drifted down from the continental shelf and slope** form the **continental rise**.

Example The United States owns its continental shelf. It extends from the continent outward 200 nautical miles into the ocean waters.

Apply Label the diagram at the right.

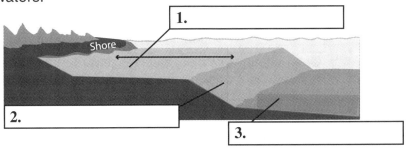

high tide / low tide

Confused Thinking The words high tide (**hī tīd**) and low tide (**lō tīd**) are confusing because the cause of the rise and fall of ocean water is not understood.

> ***Amazing Fact***
> *Isaac Newton was the first person to scientifically explain ocean **tides**.*

Straight Talk The rise and fall in sea level with respect to the land is called tides. When the **water is at its highest level** we say there is a **high tide**. When the **water is at its lowest level**, there is a **low tide**. Tides change from high to low every six hours.

Example The gravitational pull between Earth and the moon causes the tides.

Apply Answer the questions below.

1. Low tide was posted on the beach at 1:00 P.M.
   When will the next high tide begin? _____
2. When will the next low tide begin? _____

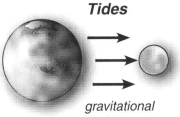

Tides

gravitational pull of the moon

Oceanography

intertidal zone / neritic zone / open ocean zone

Confused Thinking The words intertidal zone (in-tər-**tī**-dəl **zōn**), neritic zone (nə-**ri**-tik **zōn**), and open-ocean zone (ō-pən-ō-shən **zōn**) are confusing because they are unfamiliar terms dealing with the ocean's life zones.

Straight Talk The ocean has three main life zones. The **intertidal zone** is part of the **shore that is between the high and low tide lines**. The **neritic zone** extends out from the intertidal zone **across the continental shelf. The open-ocean zone** is part of the ocean **above the continental slope and the deep ocean floor**.

Example

Zone	Organisms	Conditions
Intertidal	star fish, sea anemones, sea cucumbers, crabs	covered by water at high tide and open to the air at low tide
Neritic	plankton, lobsters sponges, fish	depth of up to 200 meters, stable temperature and salinity levels
Open-ocean	whales, dolphins, swordfish, seals, and tuna	depths of up to 6,000 meters, temperatures in deepest part are just above freezing, and water pressure increases greatly with depth

Apply Label each ocean zone in the diagram.

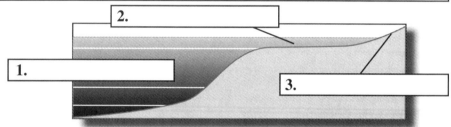

nekton / plankton / benthos

Confused Thinking The words nekton (**nek**-tən), plankton (**plangk**-tən), and benthos (**ben**-thos), are confusing because they are unfamiliar terms dealing with organisms that live in the ocean.

Straight Talk Three groups of organisms live in the ocean's neritic zone. **Nektons** are **free-swimming organisms** found at all water depths in the neritic zone. **Plankton** are organisms that **float at or near the surface** of the ocean water. A **benthos** is an organism that **lives on the ocean floor**.

> **Amazing Fact**
> A lobster, a **benthos** organism, breathes through its legs. It takes in water through its legs and lets it out through its head.

Example Salmon and sharks are part of the nekton group. Plankton include algae and krill. The benthos group includes clams and sponges.

Apply Explain why salmon and sharks are classified as nekton organisms. _____
_____

Oceanography

spring tides / neap tides

Confused Thinking The words spring tides (**spring tīdz**) and neap tides (**nēp tīdz**) are confusing because the relationship between the sun, moon, and earth is not understood.

Straight Talk The pull on Earth by the sun and moon causes the rise and fall in sea levels. Twice a month, the sun, earth, and moon form a straight line in space. Both the sun and the moon pull on the earth causing **spring tides**. During this time, **high tides are higher than usual and low tides are lower than usual**. When the earth, moon, and sun are at right angles to each other, **low tides are not very low and high tides are not very high**. These are called **neap tides**. These tides are not as great because the pull of the sun decreases the moon's pull on the earth.

Example

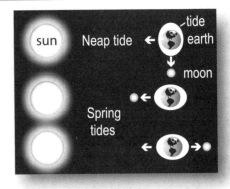

Apply Complete the data table. Fill in the cause and effect of each type of tide.

Tide	Cause	Effect
spring tide		
neap tide		

surface currents / subsurface currents

Confused Thinking The words surface currents (**sər-fəs kər-ənts**) and subsurface currents (**səb-sər-fəs kər-ənts**) are confusing because the concept of ocean currents is not understood.

Straight Talk Water density changes with both temperature and salinity. This causes motion beneath the waves called currents, which are essentially rivers of water that flow throughout the oceans. There are two types of ocean currents. **Surface currents are the result of wind blowing over the ocean's surface. Subsurface currents are rivers of cold salty water that flow deep in the ocean.** They are the result of denser, cold, salty water sinking below the less dense, warm and less salty water of the surface currents.

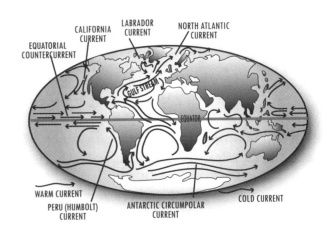

Apply Explain why deep ocean currents are colder and saltier than surface currents. _____

Oceanography

trade winds / prevailing westerlies / polar easterlies

Confused Thinking The words trade winds (**trād winds**), prevailing westerlies (pri-**vāl**-ing wes-tər-lēz), and polar easterlies (**pō**-lər ē-stər-lēz) are confusing because the creation and movement of air is not understood.

Straight Talk Earth's air masses break up into cells that result in certain consistent wind patterns. The **trade winds** occur between **latitudes of 30 degrees north and south. These warm winds blow back toward the equator** from east to west in usually clear skies. The **prevailing westerlies** occur between **40 degrees and 60 degrees north and south latitudes**, consisting of cool air usually moving quickly **toward the poles from west to east** in both hemispheres. The **polar easterlies** occur between **60 and 90 degrees north and south latitudes**; this is **cold polar air blowing from east to west**.

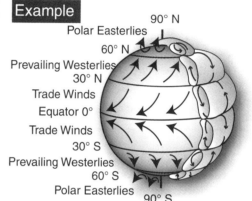

Example

90° N
Polar Easterlies
60° N
Prevailing Westerlies
30° N
Trade Winds
Equator 0°
Trade Winds
30° S
Prevailing Westerlies
60° S
Polar Easterlies
90° S

Apply Answer the questions below.

1. Which winds occur between 40 and 60 degrees north and south latitudes?

_____

2. Which winds blow back toward the equator?

_____

 Check Yourself

Matching

1. _____ neap tides
2. _____ surface currents
3. _____ trade winds
4. _____ continental shelf
5. _____ Isaac Newton

a. land near the shoreline covered with water
b. blow back toward the equator from east to west
c. occurs when the earth, moon, and sun are at right angles to each other in space
d. first to scientifically explain ocean tides
e. a result of wind blowing over the ocean's surface

Fill in the Blanks

tides	plankton	neritic	six	subsurface

6. The gravitational pull between Earth and the moon causes the _____.
7. The _____ zone extends across the continental shelf.
8. Algae and krill that float at or near the surface of the ocean water are classified as

_____.

9. The tides change from high to low every _____ hours.
10. Cold, salty water that flows deep in the ocean forms _____ currents.

Meteorology

air pressure / barometric pressure

Confused Thinking The words air pressure (**âr presh**-ər) and barometric pressure (ber-ə-**me**-trik **presh**-ər) are confusing because they are two terms used to refer to the same science concept.

Straight Talk **Air pressure** is a measure of the **weight of air pressing down on a given area of Earth's surface**. Air pressure is caused by the weight of air from the top of the atmosphere pressing down on the layers of air below. Meteorologists use **an instrument called a barometer to measures changes in air pressure**. When they read a barometer, they call that measurement **barometric pressure**. Barometric pressure and air pressure are the same thing.

> **Amazing Fact**
> *Before barometers were invented, meteorologists used frogs to predict air pressure changes. Frogs croak when the **barometric pressure** drops.*

Example

Barometric Pressure	Weather
falling air pressure	warmer, wetter weather
sudden fall in air pressure	stormy weather is on its way
air pressure rises	fair weather is on its way
air pressure is steady	no change in weather

Apply Answer the questions below.
1. Friday was sunny and warm. Saturday morning, the barometric pressure falls. What is the weather most likely going to be the rest of the day? _____

2. This morning the weather is sunny and warm. The barometric pressure is steady. What is the weather most likely going to be for the rest of the day? _____

climate / weather

Confused Thinking The words climate (**klī**-mit) and weather (**we***th*-ər) are confusing because the relationship between the two terms is not understood.

Straight Talk **Climate** is the **average weather pattern of a region** over a long period of time. **Weather** is **the condition of the atmosphere at a particular time and place** in a region. Weather is determined by four factors: heat energy, air pressure, winds, and moisture.

Example World Climate Zones

Apply Read each statement and decide if weather or climate is being described.
1. The summers in Missouri are warm and humid. _____
2. Stratus clouds presently cover the entire sky. _____
3. April is our rainiest month. _____

Meteorology

cold front / warm front

Confused Thinking The words cold front (**kōld frunt**) and warm front (**wôrm frunt**) are confusing because the relationship between the movement of cold and warm air masses and weather is not understood.

Straight Talk Weather fronts are where active weather occurs. Fronts are found along leading edges of air masses. The temperature and pressure of the air mass dictates the name of the front. If a **cold air mass overtakes a warm mass**, a **cold front** is created. Typically, cold, dense air plows under warm, moist air, causing it to rise rapidly. Such a front is likely to yield a sudden, heavy, rain shower followed with fair, cooler weather. If a **warm air mass overtakes a cold air mass**, a **warm front** is created. The less dense, warm air slides over the heavy, dense, cooler air. Stratus clouds often develop along with longer periods of steady rainfall. It is followed by warmer, more humid weather.

Example

A cold front usually moves   A warm front usually moves
from northwest to southeast.   from southwest to northeast.

Apply It is a hot summer day. A cold front moves in, bringing violent storms. What would you expect the weather to be after the storm? _____

dew point / frost point

Confused Thinking The words dew point (**do͞o point**) and frost point (**frôst point**) are confusing because both are formed by moisture in the air.

Straight Talk **Dew point** is the **temperature at which the moisture in the air begins to condense. Frost point** is the **temperature at which the moisture in the air begins to condense and ice is formed** instead of dew.

Example

Dew on a spider web.   Frost on a spider web.

Apply Put some ice and water into a tin can. Place a thermometer in the can. (Do not stir the mixture with the thermometer.) When water droplets form on the outside of the can, measure the temperature of the ice/water mixture. This temperature is the dew point. Dew is formed when water vapor in the air changes to drops by coming in contact with the cold air.

Meteorology

heat / temperature

Confused Thinking The words heat (**hēt**) and temperature (**tem**-pər-ə-chŏŏr) are often confused because they are commonly misused in everyday language.

Straight Talk **Heat** is the **transfer of energy from one object to a cooler object**. When heat is added to an object, the temperature rises. **Temperature** is the **measure of the average kinetic energy of the individual particles of a substance**. Fast-moving molecules in a substance mean a higher temperature. Heating an object causes the molecules to move faster.

Example Temperature is expressed in degrees (°). The Fahrenheit (°F) and Celsius (°C) temperature scales are the two most common scales used in science classrooms and on thermometers. Most thermometers have both scales.

Apply Complete the data table. Identify each description as an example of heat or temperature.

Description	Heat or Temperature?
1. measuring with a thermometer	
2. a pot of water begins to boil	
3. a spoon becomes warm in a cup of hot soup	

humidity / relative humidity

Confused Thinking The words humidity (hyŏŏ-**mid**-i-tē) and relative humidity (**rel**-ə-tiv hyŏŏ-**mid**-i-tē) are confusing because the concepts are closely related.

Straight Talk **Humidity** is a **measure of the amount of water vapor in a given mass of air**. Air at different temperatures is capable of holding varying amounts of moisture. **Relative humidity** is the **amount of water an air mass is holding relative to the maximum amount it could hold when completely saturated**. Relative humidity is measured and reported as a percentage. Air saturated with water vapor has a relative humidity of 100%.

Example Our skin releases moisture into the air to cool and maintain our body temperature. It is very sensitive to humidity. When the relative humidity is high, we feel much hotter than the actual temperature because moisture from our skin will not evaporate easily. When the relative humidity is low, our sweat evaporates easily, cooling us off. As a result, we feel much cooler than the actual temperature.

> **Amazing Fact**
> *Our planet's atmosphere can hold as much as 14 million tons of water at any give time.*

Apply How will your body react on a day when the air temperature is 85°F (24°C) and the relative humidity is 98 percent? _____

_____

Meteorology

high pressure system / low pressure system

Confused Thinking The words high pressure system (hī **presh**-ər **sis**-təm) and low pressure system (lō **presh**-ər **sis**-təm) are confusing because the idea that wind or moving air is a result of the difference in air pressure is not understood.

Straight Talk **Regions of sinking cool air** are called **high pressure systems**. Clear skies and fair weather usually occur in these regions. Winds rotate clockwise in the northern hemisphere, and counterclockwise in the southern hemisphere in a high pressure system. **Regions of rising warm moist air** are called **low pressure systems**. Clouds, rain, or snow and strong winds often occur in these regions. In a low pressure system, the winds rotate counterclockwise. If the pressure is very low, these spiralling winds may reach storm or hurricane force.

Example High Pressure System    Low Pressure System (hurricane)

Apply Complete the data table. Describe the wind and weather for each system.

Pressure System	Wind Direction	Weather
high pressure system		
low pressure system		

hurricane / tornado

Confused Thinking The words hurricane (**hûr**-i-kān) and tornado (tôr-**nā**-dō) are confusing because both are powerful storms.

Straight Talk **Hurricanes** form **powerful storms over tropical oceans** near the North and South Americas in the Atlantic or eastern Pacific Oceans. Hurricanes in the Atlantic always move towards the west and spin in a counterclockwise direction about the eye, or center, of the storm. The eyes are calm, while around them air speeds can reach up to 480 km/h. **Violent, whirling funnel clouds over land** are called **tornadoes**. They form in low cumulonimbus clouds. Tornadoes rotate counterclockwise in the northern hemisphere and clockwise in the southern hemisphere. They cause great damage with winds that spin up to 95 km/h.

Apply Label each diagram as an illustration of a tornado or hurricane.

Example Hurricanes are named storms that can last for days. Hurricane Katrina caused billions of dollars of damage when it hit New Orleans and surrounding areas. Tornadoes are parts of thunderstorms that last a few minutes. Tornadoes often occur across parts of Texas, Oklahoma, and Kansas known as Tornado Alley.

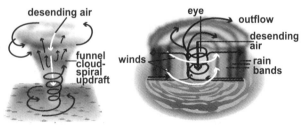

1. _____   2. _____

Meteorology

hydrologic cycle / water cycle

Confused Thinking The words hydrologic cycle (hī-drə-**loj**-ik **sī**-kəl) and water cycle (**wôt**-ər **sī**-kəl) are confusing because they are commonly used terms for the same concept.

Straight Talk The amount of water on the earth has remained the same since its formation. **Hydrologic cycle** is another name for **water cycle**; the cycle is an **exchange of water between land, bodies of water, and the atmosphere**. Water moves from the land to the atmosphere in the repeated process of evaporation, condensation, and precipitation.

> **Word Clue**
> *hydro* - a prefix meaning **water**

Example Evaporation occurs when the sun heats up water in rivers, lakes, or the ocean and turns it into vapor or steam. Eventually, it condenses and falls back to the earth as precipitation, and the cycle starts again.

Apply Label the parts of the water cycle in the diagram.

✓ Check Yourself

Matching

1. _____ climate
2. _____ hurricanes
3. _____ high pressure system
4. _____ cold front
5. _____ hydrologic cycle

a. cold air mass overtakes a warm mass
b. region of sinking cool air
c. storms over tropical oceans
d. the average weather pattern for a region
e. process of evaporation, condensation, and precipitation

Fill in the Blanks

counterclockwise	frost	warm	barometer	tornado

6. Meteorologists use a _____ to measure changes in air pressure.
7. A _____ front usually moves from southwest to northeast.
8. The temperature at which the moisture in the air begins to condense and ice is formed instead of dew is called the _____ point.
9. A violent, whirling, funnel cloud over land is called a _____.
10. The winds of a hurricane rotate _____.

Astronomy

asteroid / comet

Confused Thinking The words asteroid (**as**-tə-roid) and comet (**kom**-it) are confusing because it is not understood that objects other than the planets move through our solar system.

Straight Talk An **asteroid** is an **irregularly shaped rock, smaller than a planet, that revolves around the sun**. Most of the asteroids orbit about midway between the orbits of Mars and Jupiter. This region of the solar system is sometimes called the asteroid belt. A **comet** is often called a dirty snowball. It is a combination of **ice, dust, and rock material that follows a long, elliptical orbit about the Sun**. A comet has a head and long, flowing vapor tail.

Apply Answer the questions below.

1. What are the characteristics of an asteroid?

   _____

   _____

2. What are the characteristics of a comet?

   _____

   _____

Example

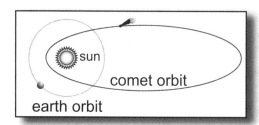

extrasolar planet / Jovian planet / terrestrial planet

Confused Thinking The words extrasolar planet (**ek**-strə-sō-lər **plan**-it), Jovian planet (**jō**-vē-ən **plan**-it), and terrestrial planet (tə-**res**-trē-əl **plan**-it) are confusing because they are unfamiliar terms.

Straight Talk The solar system consists of the sun and the bodies that are in orbit around it. There are eight planets in our solar system. The **terrestrial** or inner belt planets are **Mercury, Venus, Earth, and Mars**. The inner belt is separated from the outer belt of planets by the asteroid belt. The outer belt includes the **Jovian Planets: Jupiter, Saturn, Uranus, and Neptune**. (Pluto is no longer considered a true planet by astronomers.) **Extrasolar planets** are **planets outside our solar system**. Most of the extrasolar planets are Jupiter-sized or larger.

Memory Trick

A mnemonic device can help you remember the ***planets***.

Mercury	My
Venus	Very
Earth	Educated
Mars	Mother
Jupiter	Just
Saturn	Served
Uranus	Us
Neptune	Nachos

Example

Apply Create a mnemonic device of your own to help you remember the planets and their order.

66

Astronomy

lunar eclipse / solar eclipse

Confused Thinking The words lunar eclipse (**loo**-nər i-**klips**) and solar eclipse (**sō**-lər i-**klips**) are confusing because the cause and effect of an eclipse are not clearly understood.

Straight Talk A **lunar eclipse** occurs when **Earth passes between the moon and the sun** casting a shadow on the moon. A **solar eclipse** is a blackout of the Sun's light when the **moon passes between the earth and the sun**. The moon's shadow extends all the way to the earth and causes a brief period of darkness for people who are under it.

Example A lunar eclipse can occur about every six months when the earth passes between the sun and moon. A partial solar eclipse can occur in the same spot every 18 years, but a total eclipse of the sun might not occur for over 370 years!

> **Amazing Fact**
> A **lunar eclipse** only occurs when the moon is full.

Apply Identify the type of eclipse shown below.

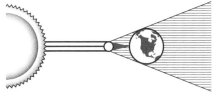
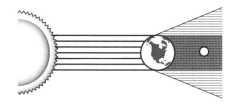

1. _____   2. _____

meteoroid / meteor / meteorite

Confused Thinking The words meteoroid (**mē**-tē-ə-roid), meteor (**mē**-tē-ôr), and meteorite (**mē**-tē-ə-rīt), are confusing because the terms sound alike and are closely related.

Straight Talk A **meteoroid** is the **space rock or dust from a comet or broken-up asteroid**. Millions of tons of meteoroids enter the earth's atmosphere each year. A **meteor** is a **streak of light formed by a meteoroid burning up as it plunges into Earth's atmosphere**. If the meteoroid **strikes Earth's surface**, it is called a **meteorite**.

> **Amazing Fact**
> A shooting star, sometimes called a falling star, has nothing to do with a star. These impressive streaks of light in the night sky are caused by small bits of dust and rock called **meteoroids** entering Earth's atmosphere.

Example Meteorites that hit the earth can create large craters.

Apply Answer the questions below.

1. Shooting stars are really _____.
2. Craters can be caused by _____.
3. Space rocks from a comet or a broken asteroid are called _____.

Astronomy

moon / satellite

Confused Thinking The words moon (**mo͞on**) and satellite (**sat**-l-īt) are confusing because the terms have similar meanings.

Straight Talk A **moon** is a **celestial body that revolves around a planet**. A **satellite** is a **small body that orbits around a larger body**. A satellite can be natural or man-made. A moon is a natural satellite of a planet.

Example The moon is Earth's natural satellite. Mars has two moons: Phobos and Deimos. There are many man-made satellites orbiting Earth.

Apply The International Space Station orbiting the earth is a satellite. Explain. _____

_____

_____

penumbra / umbra

Confused Thinking The words penumbra (pi-**num**-brə) and umbra (**um**-brə) are confusing because they are an unfamiliar word pair.

Straight Talk During an eclipse, a shadow is created by the earth or the moon. There are two parts to the shadow: penumbra and umbra. The **penumbra** is **an outer cone of partial shadow**, which diverges away from the earth or moon, instead of tapering. The **umbra** is **a central cone of darkness**, which tapers away from the earth or moon.

Example

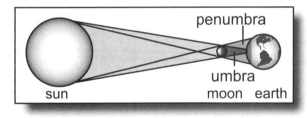

Apply Label the parts of the shadow cast by the earth during a lunar eclipse.

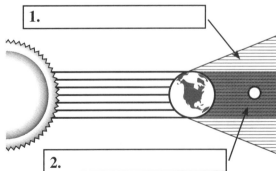

1. _____

2. _____

Astronomy

rotation / revolution

Confused Thinking The words rotation (rō-**tā**-shən) and revolution (rev-ə-**lo͞o**-shən) are confusing because the movement of planets in space is not understood.

Straight Talk The two main movements of a planet are rotation and revolution. The **rotation, or spinning,** of a planet **on its axis,** an invisible line drawn between its north and south poles, **results in days and nights** on the planet's surface. A planet revolves around the sun in a yearly cycle that produces the seasons. One **revolution,** or **orbit, of a planet around the sun in a yearly cycle** produces seasons.

Example Earth rotates west to east on its axis once every 24 hours. The earth is rotating on its axis at about 1,000 miles an hour. At the same time, the earth is moving around our sun at about 67,000 miles per hour. Earth makes one revolution around the sun once every 365 days; this makes a year.

Apply At dawn, the sun appears in the eastern sky. Explain. _____

_____

Looking at the sky from Earth, the sun, moon, planets, and stars all rise in the east and set in the west. That's because Earth spins on its axis toward the east.

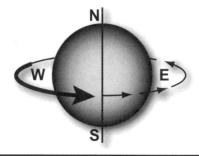

star / sun

Confused Thinking The words star (**stär**) and sun (**sun**) are confusing because the two terms refer to the same type of celestial body.

Straight Talk A **star** is a **ball of gas that produces energy in its core by means of nuclear reactions.** A **sun** is the **star at the center of a solar system.**

> **Amazing Fact**
> The **sun** is 93 million miles away from Earth, so by the time sunlight reaches Earth, the light is eight minutes old.

Example Scientists believe that a star comes into being, exists for awhile, and then dies. A star begins its life as a huge spinning cloud of dust and gas called a nebula. Gravity pulls the cloud of gas and dust together into a spinning ball. As this happens, the temperature of the cloud rises, causing the hydrogen to begin to change into helium. This produces great amounts of nuclear energy. The cloud begins to glow, and a star is born. Eventually, the supply of hydrogen is used up. After it has exhausted its nuclear fuel, a star such as our sun collapses and becomes a white dwarf. The white dwarf slowly cools over billions of years, eventually fading to near invisibility as a black dwarf.

Apply Why do scientists believe our sun may eventually become a black dwarf? _____

_____

Astronomy

solstice / equinox

Confused Thinking The words solstice (**sōl**-stis) and equinox (**ē**-kwə-noks) are confusing because the relationship between the tilt of Earth on its axis and the changing of the seasons is not understood.

Example

Straight Talk The revolution of the earth around the sun and the tilt of the earth on its axis cause the seasons. The **solstice is the point at which the sun is farthest north or south of the equator** because of the tilt of Earth. December 20th or 21st is the first day of winter in the Northern Hemisphere. Known as the winter solstice, this day has the fewest hours of daylight out of any day of the year. June 20th or 21st is the summer solstice. The Northern Hemisphere is tilted toward the sun and

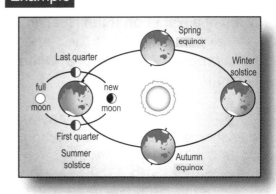

receives the most daylight. The **equinox** occurs two times a year when the **earth receives direct sunlight at the equator**. There are equal hours of sunlight and darkness on the equinoxes. March 20th or 21st is the first day of spring. It is also called the vernal equinox. September 20th or 21st is the first day of autumn. It is also called the autumnal equinox.

Apply If it is winter in the Northern Hemisphere, what season is it in the Southern Hemisphere? Explain. _____

_____

telescope / microscope

Confused Thinking The words telescope (**tel**-ə-skōp) and microscope (**mī**-krə-skōp) are often confused because the reason for using each instrument is not understood.

Straight Talk A **telescope** is an instrument used for **viewing faraway objects**, such as planets and stars. A **microscope** is an instrument used to **view small objects** that can't be seen with the naked eye. A microscope can be used to observe the microorganisms in a sample of pond water.

> *Word Clue*
> *tele* - a prefix meaning *far off*
> *micro* - a prefix meaning *small*
> *scope* - a base word meaning *to view*

Example

Apply Fill in the blanks below.

1. A scientist would use a _____ to examine white blood cells attacking bacteria.

2. A scientist would use a _____ to observe a crater on the moon.

Microscope   Telescope

Astronomy

waxing / waning

Confused Thinking The words waxing (**waks**-ing) and waning (**wān**-ing) are confusing because the names of the phases of the moon during a lunar month are not familiar terms.

Example

Straight Talk The light we see from the moon is reflected sunlight. One side of the moon always faces the sun. When the moon moves around the earth, we can't always see the lighted side of the moon. As a result, the moon seems to change shape. When the moon's entire lighted surface faces away from the earth, it is a new moon. During the first seven days after a new moon, the moon becomes a **waxing** crescent, or **enlarging or expanding** crescent. After one-quarter revolution, you can see half the moon's face. This is the first quarter moon. As the moon moves farther along its path around Earth, more and more of its face becomes visible, forming the waxing gibbous moon. Finally, when the moon reaches the spot where Earth lies between it and the sun, all of its face is illuminated as a full moon. As the moon continues to move, the area visible becomes less and less, creating the **waning** gibbous moon, or **shrinking or disappearing** gibbous moon, the last quarter, and the waning crescent moon.

New Moon

Waxing Crescent

First Quarter

Waxing Gibbous

Full Moon

Waning Gibbous

Second Quarter

Waning Crescent

New Moon

Apply In which phase is the moon invisible? _____

Check Yourself

Matching

1. _____ comet
2. _____ extrasolar planets
3. _____ solar eclipse
4. _____ revolution
5. _____ star

a. planets outside our solar system
b. moon passes between the earth and the sun
c. one orbit of a planet around the sun
d. dirty snowball of ice, dust, and rock
e. sun

Fill in the Blanks

| solstice | waxing | penumbra | comet | telescope |

6. During the winter _____, the Northern Hemisphere is tilted away from the sun.
7. A scientist would use a _____ to observe the rings of Uranus.
8. After a new moon, the moon becomes a _____ crescent.
9. A shadow produced during an eclipse has two parts: _____ and umbra.
10. A _____ has a head and long, flowing, vapor tail.

Index

Index (cont.)

Answer Keys

Pronunciation Keys (page 5)
Pronunciation Keys (page 5)
1. 5   2. second   3. oil   4. come   5. fur

Chapter 1—Physical Science
Section: Matter
atomic mass / atomic number (page 6)
1. atomic number 13, atomic mass 26.982
2. atomic number 8, atomic mass 15.999
3. atomic number 2, atomic mass 4.003
chemical / covalent / ionic bond (page 6)
Water is an example of a covalent bond.
Hydrogen shares an electron with oxygen.
element / molecule / compound (page 7)
1. molecule; the smallest unit of the compound water
2. element, a pure substance (neon) made of atoms of the same type
3. compound, formed when two or more different atoms join together chemically
mass / weight (page 7)
A person would weigh less on the moon because the gravitational pull of the moon is less than on Earth. The mass of a person would stay the same because mass does not change with location.
Check Yourself (page 8)
1. b   2. a   3. e   4. d   5. c
6. element   7. compound   8. newtons
9. nucleus   10. chemical

Section: Chemistry
acid / base / neutral (page 9)
1. acid   2. neutral   3. base
carbon dioxide / carbon monoxide (page 9)
The yeast and water mixture form carbon dioxide gas.
chemical / physical change (page 10)
1. physical   2. chemical   3. physical   4. chemical
chemical equation / formula (page 10)
1. formula   2. equation   3. equation
endothermic / exothermic reaction (page 11)
1. endothermic   2. exothermic
heterogeneous / homogeneous (page 11)
1. heterogeneous   2. homogeneous
3. homogeneous   4. heterogeneous
soluble / dissolved (page 12)
The powder dissolves in the water as the particles fall.
solute / solvent (page 12)
1. water, carbon dioxide   2. water, salt
3. gas, gas   4. zinc, copper
solution / suspension (page 13)
suspension, The particles are large enough to see. The chocolate appears to be well mixed at first, but after awhile, it settles to the bottom of the glass.
Check Yourself (page 13)
1. c   2. e   3. d   4. b   5. a
6. homogeneous mixture   7. dissolved

8. solute   9. suspension   10. chemical formula

Section: Force and Motion
balanced forces / unbalanced forces (page 14)
1. unbalanced   2. balanced
centrifugal force / centripetal force (page 14)
1. centripetal   2. centrifugal
simple / compound machines (page 15)
1. compound   2. simple
3. compound   4. simple
speed / acceleration / velocity (page 16)
1. velocity   2. speed   3. acceleration
Check Yourself (page 16)
1. e   2. c   3. b   4. a   5. d
6. Third   7. First   8. simple machine
9. compound machine   10. Acceleration

Section: Energy
conduction / convection / radiation (page 17)
1. radiation   2. convection   3. conduction
kinetic energy / potential energy (page 18)
1. kinetic   2. potential
mechanical / electromagnetic wave (page 18)
1. mechanical   2. electromagnetic
3. electromagnetic   4. mechanical
work / power (page 19)
1. work   2. power   3. power   4. work
Check Yourself (page 19)
1. d   2. e   3. b   4. c   5. a
6. mechanical 7. potential   8. work
9. convection 10. x-ray

Section: Waves, Sound, and Light
absorption / transmission (page 20)
1. transmission   2. absorption
amplitude / loudness (page 20)
1. 4 cm, The amplitude is the distance from rest position to a trough or crest.
concave lens / convex lens (page 21)
1. convex   2. concave
crest / trough (page 21)
1. crest   2. trough
diffraction / interference (page 22)
1. diffraction   2. interference
frequency / pitch (page 22)
1. empty glass, fullest glass; When you tap each glass, it makes the glass vibrate. The pitch of the note depends on the amount of water in the glass. With more water, the pitch of the note is lower.
longitudinal / transverse waves (page 23)
1. transverse   2. longitudinal
opaque / translucent / transparent (page 23)
1. opaque   2. translucent
3. transparent 4. transparent

reflection / refraction (page 24)
1. refraction   2. reflection
3. refraction   4. reflection
Check Yourself (page 24)
1. d   2. e   3. c   4. a   5. b
6. transmission   7. amplitude   8. convex
9. trough   10. transparent

Section: Electricity and Magnetism
alternating current / direct current (page 25)
1. direct   2. alternating
attraction / repulsion (page 25)
1. repel   2. attract   3. repel   4. attract
conductor / insulator (page 26)
1. insulator   2. conductor   3. insulator
4. insulator   5. conductor   6. conductor
electric circuit / electric current (page 26)
1. electric current   2. electric circuit
electricity / magnetism (page 27)
Electricity and magnetism are closely related.
Every electric current has its own magnetic field.
This magnetic force can be used to make an
electromagnet.
magnetic field / magnetic force (page 27)

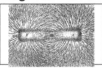

series circuit / parallel circuit (page 28)
1. series   2. parallel
Check Yourself (page 28)
1. c   2. a   3. e   4. b   5. d
6. parallel   7. amps   8. conductor
9. direct   10. attract

Chapter 2—Life Science
Section: Structure of Life
cell cycle / cytokinesis (page 29)
Cytokinesis occurs during telophase of the cell cycle.
diffusion / osmosis (page 30)
The skin of the balloon and cell membrane both have
small pores that allow molecules to pass through.
eukaryotic cell / prokaryotic cell (page 30)
1. eukaryotic   2. prokaryotic
3. prokaryotic   4. eukaryotic
multicellular / unicellular (page 31)
Multicellular - organisms made up of many cells,
    snails, fish, trees, humans
Unicellular - organism with only one cell, bacteria
Both - all organisms are made of cells
Check Yourself (page 31)
1. b   2. e   3. c   4. d   5. a
6. telophase   7. plant   8. diffusion
9. prokaryotic 10. multicellular

Section: Classification
amphibian / reptile (page 32)
1. amphibian   2. reptile
autotroph / heterotroph (page 33)
1. heterotroph   2. autotroph
3. autotroph   4. heterotroph
cold-blooded / warm-blooded (page 33)
1. cold-blooded   2. warm-blooded
3. cold-blooded   4. warm-blooded
dicot / monocot (page 34)
1. dicot   2. monocot   3. monocot   4. dicot
endoskeleton / exoskeleton (page 35)
1. endoskeleton   2. exoskeleton
**gravitropism / phototropism / thigmotropism
(page 35)**
1. phototropism   2. gravitropism
3. thigmotropism
innate behaviors / learned behaviors (page 36)
1. learned   2. innate   3. innate   4. learned
phloem / xylem (page 36)
The food coloring moved through the xylem tissue up
the stalk of the celery to the leaves.
respiration / transpiration (page 37)
Respiration - carbon dioxide is taken in and oxygen is
    released through the leaf
Both - part of the photosynthesis process, both occur
    in the leaf of the plant
Transpiration - water released into the atmosphere
    through the leaf
vascular / nonvascular (page 37)
1. nonvascular   2. vascular   3. nonvascular
4. vascular   5. vascular   6. nonvascular
vertebrate / invertebrate (page 38)
1. vertebrate   2. invertebrate
3. vertebrate   4. invertebrate
Check Yourself (page 38)
1. c   2. d   3. e   4. b   5. a
6. thigmotropism   7. learned   8. phloem
9. transpiration   10. vertebrate

Section: Life Cycle
asexual / sexual reproduction (page 39)
1. asexual   2. sexual
3. asexual   4. asexual
While tulips, potatoes, and strawberries do produce
seeds, they most commonly reproduce with asexual
methods.
complete / incomplete metamorphosis (page 40)
1. complete   2. incomplete
larva / pupa (page 40)
1. caterpillar   2. chrysalis
Check Yourself (page 41)
1. c   2. b   3. d   4. a   5. e
6. asexual   7. angiosperm   8. spore
9. caterpillar   10. complete

Section: Reproduction and Heredity
gene / chromosome (page 42)
The chromosomes are located in the nucleus of the cell. The genes on the chromosome carry the hereditary instructions for the cell.
genotype / phenotype (page 43)
TT, Tt, tt; tall
identical twins / fraternal twins (page 43)
fraternal twins, The fraternal twins' genetic connection is the same as siblings born at separate times. They can be of the opposite sex.
mitosis / meiosis (page 44)
1. repair and growth
2. sex cells, reproductive cells, or egg and sperm cells are all acceptable answers
Check Yourself (page 44)
1. c   2. d   3. b   4. a   5. e
6. identical   7. chromosomes   8. gene
9. reproductive   10. DNA

Section: Ecology
abiotic factor / biotic factor (page 45)
1. biotic   2. abiotic   3. abiotic   4. biotic
climax / pioneer community (page 45)
Pioneer organisms such as grasses will return, eventually animals return, and given sufficient amount of time, a new community will form. Finally, a stable community of plants and animals will remain with little change for years.
commensalism / mutualism / parasitism (page 46)
The relationship between the two organisms benefits both. The wrasse fish gets its food from cleaning the larger fish, and the larger fish stays healthy.
food chain / food web (page 46)
1. The spider, worm, and beetle populations would increase because the animal feeding on them is no longer part of the food web.
2. sun
grassland / savanna (page 47)
Answers may vary but might include the following:
1. dry in winter and wet in summer; tall stiff grasses, clumps of trees; giraffes, zebras, jackals, lions
2. dry areas; mostly short grasses; antelope, bison, wolves, coyotes
3. dry with some moisture; tall grasses; jackrabbits, deer, quail, prairie dogs
habitat / niche (page 47)
1. soil; decomposer
2. forest, deserts, and plains; scavengers feed on carcasses of dead animals
3. anywhere there are flowering plants such as a forest; pollination
4. ocean; cleaning other fish
herbivore / carnivore / omnivore (page 48)
1. omnivore   2. carnivore   3. herbivore

producer / consumer / decomposer (page 49)
1. consumer   2. producer   3. decomposer
organism / population / community (page 49)
organism - a living thing
population - all the organisms of one species
community - living and nonliving things in the ecosystem
taiga / tundra (page 50)
Answers may vary but might include the following
1. Description - cold winters and cool summers, and it stretches across a large portion of Canada, Europe, and Asia.
Plants - conifers such as cedars, firs, pines, redwoods, and spruce
Animals - woodpeckers, hawks, moose, bear, weasels, lynx, fox, wolves, deer, hares, chipmunks, shrews, and bats
2. Description - winter is long and severe, no true seasons, treeless plain in arctic regions, ground frozen all year
Plants - low shrubs, sedges, reindeer mosses, liverworts, lichens, and grasses
Animals - hares, rodents, wolves, bears, deer, caribou, musk oxen, wolverines, arctic foxes, polar bears, snowshoe rabbits, lemmings, black flies, deer flies, mosquitoes, harlequin ducks, sandpipers
Check Yourself (page 50)
1. b   2. c   3. a   4. e   5. d
6. bear   7. prey   8. consumers
9. population   10. taiga

Chapter 3—Earth and Space Science
Section: Geology
chemical / mechanical weathering (page 51)
1. mechanical   2. chemical
continental drift / plate tectonics (page 51)
1. plate tectonics
2. A supercontinent called Pangaea broke apart, forming seven plates. The motion of magma in the plastic-like layer, just under the crust, caused the movement of the plates to their present positions.
crust / mantle / core (page 52)
1. crust   2. mantle
3. outer core   4. inner core
crystal / mineral / rock (page 52)
cubic
erosion / weathering (page 53)
1. erosion   2. weathering   3. erosion
4. weathering   5. weathering
extrusive / intrusive igneous rocks (page 53)
1. lava   2. magma
focus / epicenter (page 54)
1. fault   2. epicenter   3. focus

folded / faulted mountains (page 54)
1. faulted   2. folded
gem / ore (page 55)
1. ore   2. gem   3. ore
igneous / sedimentary / metamorphic (page 55)
1. metamorphic   2. igneous
lava / magma (page 56)
fire, magma, lava
Check Yourself (page 56)
1. d   2. c   3. a   4. e   5. b
6. lava   7. magma   8. sedimentary
9. ores   10. focus

Section: Oceanography
continental shelf / slope / rise (page 57)
1. continental shelf   2. continental slope
3. continental rise
high tide / low tide (page 57)
1. 7:00 P.M.   2. 1 A.M.
intertidal / neritic / open-ocean zone (page 58)
1. open-ocean   2. neritic   3. intertidal
nekton / plankton / benthos (page 58)
They are free-swimming organisms.
spring tides / neap tides (page 59)
1. sun, Earth, and moon form a straight line in space; high tides are higher than usual and low tides are lower than usual
2. Earth, moon, and sun are at right angles to each other; low tides are not very low and high tides are not very high
surface / subsurface currents (page 59)
Denser, cold, salty water sinks below the less dense, warm and less salty water of the surface currents.
trade winds / prevailing westerlies / polar easterlies (page 60)
1. prevailing westerlies   2. trade winds
Check Yourself (page 60)
1. c   2. e   3. b   4. a   5. d
6. tides   7. neritic   8. plankton
9. six   10. subsurface

Section / Meteorology
air pressure / barometric pressure (page 61)
1. warm and wet   2. no change in the weather
climate / weather (page 61)
1. climate   2. weather   3. climate
cold front / warm front (page 62)
fair, cooler weather
heat / temperature (page 63)
1. temperature   2. heat   3. heat
humidity / relative humidity (page 63)
You will feel hot because the moisture from your skin will not evaporate easily.

high / low pressure system (page 64)
1. clockwise in the northern hemisphere, counterclockwise in the southern hemisphere; clear, cool weather
2. counterclockwise; heavy precipitation, overcast conditions, storms, tornadoes, and hurricanes
hurricane / tornado (page 64)
1. tornado   2. hurricane
hydrologic cycle / water cycle (page 65)
1. precipitation   2. condensation
3. evaporation
Check Yourself (page 65)
1. d   2. c   3. b   4. a   5. e
6. barometer   7. warm   8. frost
9. tornado   10. counterclockwise

Section: Astronomy
asteroid / comet (page 66)
1. irregularly shaped rock, smaller than a planet; most orbit midway between the orbits of Mars and Jupiter
2. ice, dust, and rock; elliptical orbit about the sun; has a head and long, flowing, vapor tail
lunar eclipse / solar eclipse (page 67)
1. solar eclipse   2. lunar eclipse
meteoroid / meteor / meteorite (page 67)
1. meteors   2. meteorites
3. meteoroids
moon / satellite (page 68)
It is a man-made object revolving around Earth.
penumbra / umbra (page 68)
1. penumbra   2. umbra
rotation / revolution (page 69)
The sun appears in the east each morning because the earth spins on its axis west to east.
star / sun (page 69)
Eventually the supply of hydrogen in the sun will be used up. The sun will collapse and become a white dwarf, then cool and fade to near invisibility as a black dwarf.
solstice / equinox (page 70)
summer; the Southern Hemisphere is tilted toward the sun
telescope / microscope (page 70)
1. microscope   2. telescope
waxing / waning (page 71)
new moon
Check Yourself (page 71)
1. d   2. a   3. b   4. c   5. e
6. solstice   7. telescope   8. waxing
9. penumbra   10. comet

Bibliography

Beaver, John B. and Don Powers. *Electricity and Magnetism: Connecting Students to Science Series.* Quincy, Illinois: Mark Twain Media, Inc., 2003.

Curtis, Mary E. and Ann Marie Longo. November 2001. *Teaching Vocabulary to Adolescents to Improve Comprehension.* International Reading Association. <http://www.readingonline.org/articles/curtis/>

Logan, LaVerne and Don Powers. *Atmosphere and Weather: Connecting Students to Science Series.* Quincy, Illinois: Mark Twain Media, Inc., 2002.

Logan, LaVerne. *Rocks and Minerals: Connecting Students to Science Series.* Quincy, Illinois: Mark Twain Media, Inc., 2002.

Logan, LaVerne. *Sound: Connecting Students to Science Series.* Quincy, Illinois: Mark Twain Media, Inc., 2002.

Marzano, Robert and Debra J. Pickering. *Building Academic Vocabulary: Teacher's Manual.* ASCD, 2005.

Marzano, Robert. *Building Background Knowledge for Academic Achievement: Research on What Works in Schools.* ASCD, 2004.

Merriam-Webster Online. 19 November 2008. <http://www.merriam-webster.com/dictionary/chromat->

Powers, Don and John B. Beaver. *The Solar System: Connecting Students to Science Series.* Quincy, Illinois: Mark Twain Media, Inc., 2004.

Project G.L.A.D. February 20, 2007. Orange County Department of Education. <http://www.projectglad.com/>

Raham, Gary. *Science Tutor: Earth and Space Science.* Quincy, Illinois: Mark Twain Media, Inc., 2006.

Raham, Gary. *Science Tutor: Life Science.* Quincy, Illinois: Mark Twain Media, Inc., 2006.

Sandall, Barbara R. *Chemistry: Connecting Students to Science Series.* Quincy, Illinois: Mark Twain Media, Inc., 2002.

Sandall, Barbara R. *Light and Color: Connecting Students to Science Series.* Quincy, Illinois: Mark Twain Media, Inc., 2004.

Sciencesaurus: A Student Handbook. Houghton Mifflin, 2002.

Science Vocabulary Strategies Handbook. 2007–2008. <www.pscubed.org/documents/CompleteBook.pdf>

Shireman, Myrl. *Physical Science.* Quincy, Illinois: Mark Twain Media, Inc., 1997.